FALLING FOR THE MOUNTAIN MAN

T. MAREE

This book was previously published in the Wilderness Mine anthology published by Fluffy Fox Publishing in April 2023.

CONTENT WARNING

This book contains adult content and sexually explicit scenes. Some scenes involve mentions of domestic abuse, self-harm, death, and stalking which may trigger some readers.

Not all possible triggers have been mentioned. By reading further, you, as the reader, are continuing with the understanding that this book is a work of fiction and that not all possible triggers may have been mentioned. The author and any who contributed to this work cannot and will not be held accountable for a reader's state of mind or actions they may take after reading this book.

OTHER BOOKS BY ME

Did you know I write under three different names?

ALEXIS MAREE

THE KINGS OF HELL SERIES:

The Kings of Hell – Cole
The Kings of Hell – Adrik
The Kings of Hell - Malik

T. MAREE

THE LEAH REYNOLDS SERIES:

Sins in the Silence
Sins of a Daughter
Sins of the Past
Sins of the Enemy
Sins of the Forbidden
Sins of the Blood

STANDALONES

Falling for the Mountain Man

LUNA MAREE

L'Amour Island
Her Sir & Sire

This book is dedicated to my partner and love of my life.
Not a single day has gone by where I have regretted falling for you.

XX

ACKNOWLEDGEMENTS

There are always so many people to acknowledge when writing a book. I'd first like to start with my friends and family, for without whom, I would lack the motivation and encouragement to keep writing.

Next, I'd like to thank Quell at Fluffy Fox Publishing, for encouraging me to join her anthology in which this book was originally published. This story wouldn't have happened without you.

To my alphas, betas, ARC readers, editors, and proofreaders, thank you SO much. You're help is truly appreciated.

Chapter One

Callan

An explosion rocked the ground beneath my feet, the heat so intense that for a moment it stole the breath from my lungs. I was thrown backwards, landing hard on sharp rocks and debris, pain radiating up my right arm and shoulder as it took the brunt of the fall. Dust coated the back of my throat as the dirt and rock exploded, and I struggled to draw in a breath. There was a ringing in my ears, my vision blurry, and my mind was temporarily paralyzed as I tried to grasp what had happened.

Shooting. Ambush. Bombs.

We were under attack. I shook away the shock, trying desperately to fall back on my training.

Move, asshole! Your team is getting torn apart out there!

The mental pep-talk was what I needed; a reminder that it wasn't just my life out here, it was theirs, too.

My brothers.

The men I stood beside as we charged into dangerous territory to complete missions we could never speak about. Most of the time, we were in and out before the enemy knew we were there. It was what we were trained for, what our purpose was.

I staggered to my feet, I steeled myself against the rush of pain and dizzying disorientation.

"Wolf!" My call sign was shouted. Was that Parker? I turned, the ringing in my ears intensifying, causing my vision to darken as I staggered blindly in the direction of my fallen teammate.

"Wolf!" Parker yelled again; this time I was sure it was him. The pain in his voice as he shouted my name jolted something inside me so that I was able to focus.

There he was, half-buried beneath some rubble, his helmet knocked from his head. I stumbled closer and dropped to my knees beside him, gritting my teeth as I shoved stone and wood away from him. He coughed. I think he was talking, but my hearing was coming and going, and that persistent ringing was making it hard to concentrate. Were the rest of my team okay? Where were they? Were we still under attack?

I checked my brother over to gauge the worst of his injuries and pressed my shaky hands onto the visible wound in his leg. Blood immediately soaked through my fingers, and I swore. "Doc!" I shouted, my voice raspy, and I coughed, struggling to wet my mouth. "Doc!"

More blood, more pain, more screaming in agony from the soldier beneath me. I shook my head as the white light behind my eyes grew brighter, the high-pitched ringing in my ears growing higher and louder. I winced and groaned, but I couldn't lift my hands, or he'd bleed out. More and more light and the high-pitched noise grew until I was roaring for it all to stop.

As if all sound had been turned off, it was suddenly quiet, and someone touched my shoulder. I lifted my head, and I was sitting crouched on the floor in a sterile, white hallway. I glanced down; I wasn't in a warzone anymore, but something was wrong, so very wrong. My brother was gone, my hands were clean of blood, and I was staring at the white floor beneath me. The hand on my shoulder tightened and I heard the soft, sympathetic voice of a woman. I shook my head, my cheeks wet with tears, my combat boots still dusty from whatever hellhole I'd just come back from. I was still wearing my uniform. I ached, but nothing hurt more than my heart.

"We're so sorry. She was hemorrhaging, and we couldn't stop the bleeding," the woman said. My head was still in my hands and once again, drawing breath was a struggle. I was immediately filled with the desire to stop breathing. What was the point of any of it anymore?

"She fought hard, and she wanted you to know she loved you. She stressed it a lot and begged you to hold on and stay strong for her," the woman continued. I shook my head, my chest constricting, my stomach an aching ball of lead.

"Cal," a soft voice called, and I looked up to see one of my teammates there, Jason, his face filled with pain, his voice thick with regret. He came to kneel in front of me so that he was my main focus. This man had been through hell with me. I'd saved his life and he'd saved mine. He'd carry this pain for me if he could, but he can't, and I wouldn't wish it on him— on anyone.

"Come and meet her, man. She needs you. If you can't live for yourself right now, live for her. She's already lost so much, and she doesn't even know it yet. I know this hurts, and I can't help take away the pain. But I'm here. The guys will be here. We'll fight to keep you on your feet, and we'll help protect that girl with our lives. But you gotta get up now, and be what she needs," Jason encouraged. This man had been my second for years, always at my back or bringing me back from the edge and getting in my face when I needed it. I trusted him with my life, with the life of anyone I cared about, which now consisted of one very tiny human I had not yet met. Did I want to fight? Did I want to continue on when my reason for coming home safe every fucking time was now

11

lifeless on a cold slab somewhere? What was even the point? A soft, sad cry rent the air and my eyes flicked behind Jason to a nurse holding a small bundle wrapped in a pink blanket. "Come meet her, man. She's all that remains of Lina. She needs you. Get up. We'll all help, we'll all be here. But you gotta get up. Don't stop fighting," Jason pushed.

I don't know where the strength came from. I honestly believe it came from Lina, reaching out to pull me to my feet for the one thing I had left here, the one person who actually needed me. It took time. My knees shook and so did my hands. My heart was in tatters, an agony unlike anything I'd ever known existed was coursing through my entire being as thick as blood, as much a part of me as my bones. It seeped into every vein and organ I possessed, but still I climbed to my feet. I got up and dragged in a ragged breath. First one, and then another, forcing it through my lungs, feeling my heart beating hard. I felt like I'd been cut in half, and now had to exist with only a part of me.

That cry sounded again, and I choked back a sob, urging myself to pull myself together. I couldn't fall apart; I couldn't break, or I'd never get back up.

I was a SEAL; we always got back up. We never stayed down, and no challenge or mission was too big to overcome. And right now, I have a new mission—my daughter.

~

My eyes opened with a snap, and my breath was trapped in my lungs, burning. I didn't fight it, I didn't panic. The pain was still there, a living, breathing entity that had been my constant companion since the day I'd lost my soulmate. I allowed it to wash over me, and I watched the rotations of the ceiling fan above me until I was finally able to draw in a slow breath. Breathing still hurt, but it wasn't the all-consuming, crippling pain it once had been. Bit by bit, my body became my own. I let my muscles relax as I sank into the mattress and breathing became easier once again. My heart still thudded hard, and when I could, I raised my hand and scrubbed it over my face.

Fuck.

Everyone always talked about moving on and moving forward, but how was it fucking possible when my every nightmare, even my dreams, were filled with visions of her? Of how we used to be when life was good? I could still smell her scent some mornings when I woke up, as if she were still here, but that was impossible. I'd moved houses after that first year and had relocated to the mountains. Being around people had been too hard, too disorienting and suffocating. I still couldn't be around them.

I scratched absently at my beard and pushed myself up, swinging my legs to the other side of the bed. It had been six years.

Six. Long. Years.

But I was still breathing. I got up every morning and I stayed on my feet. I fought every fucking day to stay here, to stay present and be all that I could be out of the tatters that had been left after I'd lost her. After I'd lost everything.

No, not everything.

"Daddy!" a distant voice sung out, accompanied by the pounding of bare feet. I smiled, the broken pieces of my heart warming as her voice grew louder and she flung open my door. My smile grew into a grin as my little wild child came flying into the room, her dark red hair tangled and curly, bouncing with every step. Her bright blue eyes shone with joy, and she hurled herself at me with the kind of self-assurance only a six-year-old could have that her father would catch her.

And I would. Every time.

I caught her tiny body and wrapped her up in my arms. She laughed and wrapped her little arms around my neck and pulled me close. My heart turned over as it always did at this absolute miracle in my arms, and for a moment, just a moment, everything was right in the world, and all the pain was gone. I closed my eyes and breathed in her little girl scent, the shampoo and soap and something that was just innocence and sunshine.

She was my reason for getting up every single day. My reason to keep breathing, to keep trying, to always keep fighting. As long as she was here, then I was here. I'd never abandon her, and I'd always, *always* protect her.

"Daddy, it's four more days till school!" she cried, her face filled with excitement.

My stomach dropped and clenched, but I forced a smile to my lips anyway.

Shit. School.

"Sure is, princess," I agreed as she wiggled out of my grasp and skipped out of my room, her red locks so much like her mother's.

I wasn't joking about my aversion to people. I'd moved into the mountains and the nearest town was forty minutes away and the roads weren't all that easy to travel which meant that it wasn't a road anyone but the most determined traveled. But Mara needed to go to school. She was six now and it was time. Besides, even *I* knew it wasn't healthy to keep her isolated and cooped up here in our mountain home for her whole life. As much as I wanted to be everything she needed, she also needed to make other connections, to be around other people and begin living her life.

Since moving here five years ago, I'd found a sense of peace in the nature that surrounded us and in the isolation the mountains provided. I'd sold our home in the city and bought five hundred and sixty acres of wilderness. Because of the rough terrain, wild animals, and isolation, I'd gotten it at a steal.

I'd realized quickly after that last mission—the one that went to hell—I had some pretty severe PTSD. The smallest things could trigger it, but it was usually when I was surrounded by people and society. I needed to stay out here to remain sane. The few times I'd been in town hadn't gone so well. Once, I'd almost hurt a random stranger. Another outing ended with me curled up in a ball on the ground trying to get cover from what I was sure were gunshots. I couldn't do it, and the thought of being around all those people again made me feel like I was suffocating.

I'd managed to make it to the outskirts of town to a park where Mara's teacher had been kind enough to meet with me so that I could see her and discuss any of my concerns or issues I had with Mara starting school. I liked her on sight. She was open and honest about everything and more than willing to work with me around any issues I had about being in town. What was more, she hadn't once tried to hit on me. It may seem arrogant, but I knew women looked at me and saw a wild night in bed. And yes, after a while, I'd taken a few of them up on it. But it had never gone past one night with any of them.

I rubbed at the muscles in the back of my neck and sighed in defeat. I *hated* that I had to ask for help. I detested needing someone for anything, but as my counselor had told me when

I'd been forced into talking about all the bullshit in the
beginning, I had to be man enough to ask for help. At first, I'd
scoffed. I was a motherfucking SEAL. We didn't ask for help,
we did things ourselves, no matter how hard. We were first in
the door, dragging others out of danger despite the risk to
ourselves. We were as tough as tough gets.

And now, I couldn't handle being in a *fucking* crowd.

It had taken a long time, and a lot of encouragement and even
orders from my brothers… but I'd finally asked for help. I'd
started with Lina's parents. I had no family left, but Lina did.
Her parents were devastated after losing her, and they'd
begged me not to cut them out of their grand-daughter's life. I
had never had an issue with my in-laws, we just rarely saw
each other. But I'd started with them. I'd asked them to take
Mara for an afternoon in the beginning, unwilling to let her
out of my sight, but needing to go back to work. I'd been put
on desk duty for the last six months of my service, and I'd
been more than happy to accept. After the shit they'd pulled
with that last mission… Well, let's just say I was having some
trust issues with the men who wrote my paycheck. When
Mara had been fine after the first afternoon with them, they'd
volunteered to take her during the day while I worked, and
graciously accepted my checking in every two hours. They'd
sent me countless photos to assure me throughout the day that
she was fine, as well as a small report on how she was doing—
If she'd eaten and so on.

The first time she stayed overnight with them, I was a
complete wreck. I'd spent the night in my car camped outside
their house. In the morning, my mother-in-law had brought
me a to-go cup with coffee in it and some breakfast and
assured me we'd see her in a few hours. They never
complained that I had trouble letting go or letting others help,

they'd been nothing but accepting.

It had been six years, and I was more easy-going now. Mara even spent some of the holidays with them and a few weekends here and there. When I'd moved here, so had they. Although, they were still far enough away that it was a decent car-ride to get to their house.

Our home was small, but we didn't need anything grand. It was a timber log-house with a few large picture windows to give a fantastic view of the wilderness that surrounded us. We were alone out here, so I wasn't all that worried about neighbors watching us all the time, but my training wouldn't allow for just any-old glass in the window frame, so I'd special ordered all the glass to be replaced with inch-thick glass-clad polycarbonate. It was the best kind of bullet-resistant glass anyone could get, and I'd paid a *lot* for it. But to me, it was worth it. I'd also had a bullet-proof panic room installed; it was by far the most secure room in the house. People can call me paranoid if they want, but I'd seen a lot of evil in the world, and I had a duty to my daughter to protect her in any way that I could. I saw my background as a SEAL as training to protect my daughter, and I'd be damned if my need for solitude made us targets for some nut-job with home-made explosives.

I'd taught Mara how to use the panic room and she knew that when I told her to hide, it meant get to the panic room. Every month we ran a drill. Sometimes it was for fires, tornadoes, strangers, or dangerous animals. Other times it was what she had to do if she was alone and hurt or if something happened to *me* and she needed help. I didn't want to scare her, but I made sure Mara understood that we were pretty much on our own out here, so we had to be prepared for it all.

We survived on tank water and solar panels. I'd had a couple of batteries installed so we weren't simply reliant on it being daylight to get power. Every time the sun shone, it powered those batteries, and we were able to use solar at night from them. Besides, we weren't huge on using technology, and Mara was in bed by seven, which meant it was just me. As long as my batteries were charged, my phone and emergency equipment were charged up, I didn't need the power. I was happy to have the fire roaring and a book, or to clean my weapons rather than watch TV.

I walked by Mara's room to check that she'd made her bed for the day. Perfect, as always. She had to be the only six-year-old who could make her bed as well as any military man. Her room was clean and orderly, and I smiled with pride. We made a game of keeping things neat in this house, and it had paid off.

I followed the sounds of her little voice singing happily in the kitchen and watched as she dragged her step stool over to the bench and then went to the fridge for the milk. Mara loved to cook, I'd discovered, and she wanted to know how to do it all. I was not a big fan of her knowing how to use the hot appliances, and even letting her use the toaster had been a huge step. I had nightmares about her sticking a fork in it and electrocuting herself, so we went over the rules of using the toaster until I was sure she knew what not to do.

She sang softly to herself one of the nursery rhymes she had on CD and measured out her breakfast cereal with the measuring cup. After many attempts to pour from the packet and ending up with a floor littered with food, I'd shown her how many scoops she needed, and this had greatly cut back on the food wastage and mess.

I poured milk into a little cup every night and put it in the fridge so she didn't have to lift a heavy carton and just had to pour the contents of the cup into the cereal bowl. She absolutely loved being independent.

It made me so proud to watch her there, confidently making her own breakfast and singing the words to her song correctly. There was a small pang in my chest at knowing she was growing up so fast, but it was the way of the world. And on the off chance something happened to me, and I wasn't around for my baby girl as long as she needed me, I was determined to teach her everything I could to make her as self-sufficient as possible. Her mother had died in childbirth, and I was her only remaining parent, the last one responsible for how she grew up and turned out. The thought of her growing into a woman who needed to rely on anyone, especially a man, to do anything, made my stomach hurt. I was sure Mara was the only first grader to know how to use a compass and how to disinfect and clean water from a wild source, and I was damned proud of her for knowing that.

But there were things I could not teach her, things that she needed to learn without me there over her shoulder, and so she had to go to school. Being around other kids more often would do her a world of good, and learning to make friends and interact with different people was necessary.

"Daddy, are we still going on our a-ven-cha?" Mara asked as she carefully carried her bowl to the table, her eyes focused so as not to spill any milk.

"We're definitely going on our adventure today, munchkin. We have a few days before you start school, so we're going to make the most of it and go camping. And Uncle Jason, Aaron, Morgan, Flynn, and Cohen will be here when we get back," I announced, referring to five of my brothers from the Navy. I was close to all my brothers, and as a result, Mara had a large number of uncles who adored her almost as much as I did.

They'd all understood my reason for leaving the team, and had been at my back ever since, visiting often and making sure Mara knew she had a big family.

"Nana and Pop?" she asked around a mouthful of food. I grinned and mussed her curly red hair as I walked past to make myself a coffee.

"Yep, they'll be here too, princess."

It was Mara's first year of school, and everyone wanted to be here to wish her luck and pass along any tips they could think of. I had a feeling this would be a yearly thing, and I was here for it. I didn't like to be around a lot of people often, but this was family, and it was for Mara, so it would never bother me to have them here.

I had just made my coffee and taken my first sip when she asked a question that had me choking and spluttering.

"Do I get a new mommy too?" she asked innocently.

It took me a minute to breathe before I could speak again, the coffee burning in my chest and nose. I cleaned up the mess and moved to kneel at her side to look at her more clearly.

"Why do you ask that?"

Mara shrugged and stared back at her bowl. "'Cause all the pictures in the school papers have a mommy and a daddy in them.".

I frowned. School papers? Obviously noticing my confusion, Mara got up and grabbed paperwork off the coffee table and brought it back to me.

I glanced down and realization dawned. All the back-to-school lists, the school brochure, and all the other crap they gave me at the parents' orientation thing had those glossy photos of two parents smiling and waving off their children.

Sighing, I scrubbed a hand over my face and tried to think how to answer her.

"Sweetheart… we've spoken about this. Not every kid has two parents. Some kids don't have a daddy, and some don't have a mommy… some don't have any parents, but that's just how the world is sometimes," I began to explain. She considered me carefully as she chewed her food, spoon in hand, and tipped her head to the side.

"If I don't get a new mommy, then you don't get a girlfriend. And if you don't get a girlfriend, then you are going to start falling apart and I don't want you to break," she told me with wide, innocent blue eyes.

"Uh… Mara, what are you talking about?" I frowned. She sighed as if I were being obtuse on purpose and set down her spoon. Oh, we were getting serious. Okay.

"When Uncle Jason and Uncle Cohen were here last time, they said if you don't get a girlfriend or get laid down soon—I don't know what that means—that your junk is going to fall off, and I just don't want any part of you to fall off even if it is junk. But I don't think any part of you is junk, Daddy," she answered seriously.

My mouth fell open and several parts of my brain tried to fire off at once, causing something of a traffic accident in my head.

"Wait, what?" I managed to wheeze, still stuck on the part where my daughter referred to my "junk".

"Your junk. Uncle Jason said—" she started.

"Wait, wait, wait. Please stop talking about my junk," I interrupted, holding up my hand and inwardly wincing at how many times she'd said it. Mara waited for me to continue, and I dragged in a deep breath, trying to find a good place to start.

"Okay, look," I began. "First of all, you should not have been listening to our conversation. That was grown-up talk, and it didn't concern you."

She pouted but waited for me to go on.

"Secondly, Uncle Jason was joking. Nothing about me is going to fall off, whether or not I find a girlfriend. And thirdly... just... don't say that word anymore," I muttered, running a hand roughly over my hair.

"Junk?"

"Yes." I winced, grinding my teeth. "And make sure you remind me to have a little talk with Uncle Jason and Uncle Cohen when we get back."

"So... you don't want a girlfriend?"

I exhaled heavily and shook my head. "No, sweetheart, I don't. Why is it bothering you?" I watched her carefully, needing to get to the root of the problem here.

Mara shrugged her little shoulders and finished what was in her bowl.

"I just don't want you to be all by yourself," she finally answered, so softly I almost missed it.

"What?" I whispered, my chest tightening at the look of sadness on her face.

"When I go to Nana's and Pop's house, you're all by yourself here. But it's only sometimes and you said sometimes grown-ups need alone time."

"Okay..." I trailed off, waiting.

She sighed. "Well, I'm going to school soon, Daddy. You will be alone all the time, not just sometimes, and it makes me sad. I don't want you to be alone." Her big blue eyes filled to the brim with worry.

"Oh sweetheart," I murmured and sat back on the ground before tugging her down onto my lap.

"I'm sad for you, Daddy. And if I get a mommy, then you won't be alone," she confessed quietly, focusing on a hole in my old shirt rather than on my face.

I squeezed her to me for a moment and kissed the top of her

head, closing my eyes.

My sweet, sweet girl.

"Mara, baby. Listen to me, darlin'," I began, hating that this had been bothering her. "I don't need to have someone here with me. I have so much to do all the time, that the whole time you're at school, I'll be busy right up until it's time to pick you up. I won't have time for anyone else, all I need is you."

"But all the other daddies will have girlfriends. And all the other kids will have mommy's," she whispered sadly. My heart clenched and I held her tiny body closer, wishing I could shield her from the knowledge she was coming to have.

"Why did Mommy have to leave?"

I closed my eyes against that familiar ache in my chest and the stinging in my eyes.

Lina, I really wish you were here.

"Hey, you remember what I told you about Mommy?" I asked, clearing my throat.

Mara nodded and leaned back to look at me with such sad eyes.

"Yes. You said that all people are made up of good stuff and bad stuff. But that Mommy was made of only good stuff. She had so much good stuff, that the universe had no more left to give to other people. So, the universe needed Mommy back so that her kindness and love could be spread all over the world," Mara said, giving me the explanation I'd given her from the first moment she'd asked about her mother.

"That's right, baby girl. And we miss her every day, but your mommy is all around, in everything good. Every time someone does something nice, or is lovely or sweet, that's your mommy right there, spreading good all around the world," I explained, my heart thudding hard in my chest.

"Will the universe ever give me another mommy?" she asked, her wide eyes beseeching.

Fuck.

"I don't know, baby. If it does, then she's going to have to be beautiful, smart, brave, honest, funny, and she is going to have to love you more than anything else in the world."

Because like hell was I ever putting my daughter in the hands of a woman who couldn't love her as if she were her own child.

"Will she need to know how to hike?" Mara asked, smiling gently.

"Definitely," I agreed with a grin, feeling relief wash over me that she was letting the subject go.

"And hunt?"

"It would be a bonus, but not absolutely needed," I joked, happy to play her game of Mommy Shopping List if it kept that sadness out of her eyes.

"What about loving nature?"

"She has to love nature, absolutely, or she won't be able to come on our hikes and she'll be bored," I answered, watching Mara as she kicked her legs lazily and thought hard for another quality.

"Will she need to make sure your junk doesn't fall off?"

I choked on my own saliva and coughed, lifting Mara so she was standing, and I was kneeling.

"Okay, enough on the Mommy Shopping List, and no more saying that word, understand?"

"Fine," she conceded with a sigh as if I were being unreasonable. "Can I ask the universe to send me a mommy if she is all the things a mommy should be?"

"Sure, baby, ask away," I agreed, getting to my feet and moving past her to the kitchen.

I dragged in a deep breath and shook my head at the turn the morning had taken.

I watched as Mara collected her spoon and bowl and put them in the sink before she skipped away to her room to start packing for our hike.

I could prepare my daughter for so much, but there were still things I would never be able to protect her from, and I wasn't sure if my heart could take seeing that heartbreaking expression on her young face again.

Sighing, I rinsed out my mug and started putting together our supplies for our camping adventure.

Chapter Two

SELINA

My muscles were screaming at me, my back was aching so badly I knew I'd be paying for it if I didn't get into a bath tonight. I wiggled my toes in my hiking boots in an attempt to get some circulation back to my legs and feet, but it wasn't enough.

Just a little longer, Selina. You can do this. Everything you've been doing for the last week has all been for this moment.

I kept repeating that to myself.

Nature photography wasn't as easy as some people thought, and especially not the shots I went for. I'd been hiking around and setting up blinds and camps over the last week, trying to get the perfect photo of a rare, native bird. They hid their nests well, and it was almost impossible to get a photo of the mother bird with her chicks. But I'd been at this a while now, and I'd found the nest. When the mother bird had left to find food, I'd set up my camp so that I was camouflaged and had been sitting here, in a tree branch for several hours now, aching to move and relieve my cramped muscles, but not daring to. She'd be back any minute, and if I moved now, she'd see and disappear for God knows how long. Then this would have been a waste of an entire week.

I was sweaty, I was dirty, and I was dying for a shower, even if it was just to wash off in the freezing mountain stream. In fact, that sounded like heaven. I let out another slow breath and tried to concentrate on anything besides how much my legs hurt.

I made a good amount of money as a nature photographer, and while I was here, I documented anything I saw regarding them. Moods, food, habits, and so on. But I didn't make enough to live off, so I also offered my services as a photographer for school photos and for weddings. That was my bread and butter, and thankfully I was requested often. I loved photography, always had, even as a young girl. I'd owned a polaroid and had spent all my pocket money to buy new film for it every week. I smiled at the memory, my heart clenching at the thought of my father. He had been a good man, a good father, always trying his best to provide for me and keep me safe. I'd been his little girl, and he'd been my whole world.

Fuck cancer.

That's all I had to say about that. Once he'd been diagnosed, I'd only gotten six more months with him before he'd faded away. At least it had been quick in the way that he hadn't had to suffer for long. And I knew he was with my mother now, finally complete and at peace. He'd loved her more than I ever knew a man to love a woman. He'd never moved on after her, instead choosing to make me his reason for living. And he'd never let me feel as though I was missing out by not knowing my mother. She'd died in a car accident, a year after I'd been born. Where other girls may have learned how to do their makeup or how to dress for an occasion or do their hair in fancy twists, I'd learned how to camp in the wilderness, how to find fresh water and food on my own. I'd learned how to shoot, although I abhorred the idea of hunting, even for food. I was too much of an animal lover, even though I could see the reason and a need for it. I just couldn't find it within myself to pull the trigger unless it was life or death. I'd learned how to drive on outback roads at ten years old, how to get myself out of car trouble, and how to fix a punctured tire and do my own services. I knew more about cars than I did about fashion, and I'd always been okay with that. My father had instilled in me a kind of confidence I'd noticed many women were missing as they grew up. That had been his legacy to me, and it was one I was proud to carry.

I was readjusting the strap of my camera when I saw her—that beautiful bird. I swallowed and slowly raised my camera as she landed on a branch only three feet from me. She was looking around, slowly hopping along the branch towards where her nest was hidden behind a kind of blind she'd created.

Honestly, these birds were fascinating. I took several shots of her moving along, and was preparing for the photo I'd been waiting hours to take, and hiked days to prepare for. She edged closer to her chicks as they chirped away with anticipation of being fed when a deafening *crack* reverberated through the air. I gasped in fright and the bird flitted away in alarm.

"Are you *kidding me?!*" I whisper-shouted to no one in particular.

A hunter.

A goddamn hunter had just ruined the shot of a lifetime. I swore under my breath and dropped my head back against the tree trunk for a moment. Fine, I'd just have to do this all over again. But not now. God no. Now, I just wanted to get out of this damned tree and get washed up and go home. I was tired, hungry, and exhausted.

I put my camera equipment back in the bag around my neck and was about to start making my way out of the tree using the rappel rope when I glanced down to see an incredibly large man step out of the brush.

I froze, my breath catching. He was a mountain, that was for sure, but he moved silently, almost too quiet. Bears and wolves weren't the only predators out here I'd been warned about. Just because he was out here, didn't mean he was a bad guy, I knew that. But I was a woman out here alone who… I inwardly groaned and looked slowly back at the bushes where I'd stashed my backpack and gun. Even my capsicum spray was in there.

I could practically hear my father's reprimand from here. *Never be caught without a way to protect yourself.*

My father had always told me to be prepared, to rely on myself and no one else. To do that, I needed to make sure I could handle any situation I might find myself in. When hiking in the woods, that included scaring off large predators.

Okay, I could just wait until he moved on before I left the tree to collect my bag. I could do that, right? I gritted my teeth and tried to ignore the painful burning in my legs and the screaming muscles in my back. I'd been in this tree too long and had just been about to leave it when he came into view. If I moved too much, he'd see me, and then I'd be trapped up here without a way to protect myself, and he had a gun.

Come on. Move, mountain man!

Breathing out slowly, I closed my eyes and concentrated on not moving and on pushing the pain away. A few more minutes wouldn't kill me, I'd be fine. I just had to grit my teeth and bear it.

The man beneath me didn't move, his eyes scanning the area, listening. My arms were beginning to shake with the effort to keep myself still and I took in slow, shallow breaths.

Finally, he turned around to go back the way he came when he stopped right beneath my tree.

"What's this?" he whispered to himself, and I turned slightly to see him looking at my bag. I gasped audibly, and his head swung up to my location, his blue eyes widening in surprise. At that moment, my arms gave out and I tumbled out of the tree.

Right on top of him.

I landed hard, and I heard his groan of pain as we slammed into the ground. Instincts kicked in, and I scrambled to my feet, hoping to put space between us but my foot caught on a root, and I fell backwards with a cry, my ankle wrenching.

"Shit!" I swore, landing hard. My ankle throbbed, pain radiating up my calf, and instant tears pricked my eyes.

"What the *hell?*" Mountain man groaned, dragging himself up to a sitting position.

I blinked the tears away angrily and sucked in a breath. Tentatively, I tried to put weight on my foot and bit back a cry of pain when stabbing pains erupted up my ankle. I took a moment to breathe deeply and think about what I was going to do. I had a first aid kit in my bag, I could try to put a compress around my ankle without removing my boot. If I could find a stick to use as a cane, I could hobble my way back to my car. It wasn't ideal, and it would take me a lot longer than usual. Although, I wondered if soaking my ankle in the cold mountain stream would help with the swelling. At least the stream was just a few feet away, so it wouldn't take me much effort to get there.

"I'm sorry," I said quickly to the man who'd broken my fall, blinking hard to get past the pain.

"Where the hell did you come from? Why were you in a goddamn tree?" he snapped, rubbing his hip and glowering at me.

"I didn't mean to fall on you, obviously," I snapped back. He stood up suddenly, towering over me, rifle in hand, and I felt the blood drain from my face when I realized the position I was in. He was an *incredibly* large, *very* muscular, *extremely* pissed off looking mountain man. I gulped as he glared down at me, his blue eyes as cold as ice. I didn't need to see through his bushy beard to know he wasn't smiling even the slightest. The man was almost the size of a bear. Like, what the hell? He took a step toward me, and I shuffled back quickly, dragging my injured leg. He paused, stopping his advances, his brow creasing.

"What the hell do you think you're doing out here?" he snarled, but he stayed back. I was momentarily stunned into silence at the fury in his voice, then my brain kicked back into gear, and I glared.

"Who the hell do *you* think you are, speaking to me like that?" I snapped, straightening my spine. I knew getting smart-mouthed with the mountain man who held a gun while I was injured was not a smart move, but my father had always said I had more temper than I did sense. Maybe he was right.

"I'm the man you just used as a landing pad. You're welcome, by the way."

"You're being rude and aggressive," I pointed out angrily.

"Says the woman snarling at me when I just saved her from breaking her wrists by landing wrong."

"I'm sorry, is there a right way to fall out of a tree?" I snarked.

"Yes—don't."

I glared in response, and he glowered right back.

"I'll ask again. What are you doing out here?" he clenched out. His tone was lowered, sending goosebumps skittering along my arms. I raised an eyebrow and crossed my arms over my chest from my very vulnerable place on the ground, contemplating not telling him. His eyes dipped to my chest for a moment before burning back onto my face and I froze. Did he just check out my *boobs*? Indignation warred with humor at the idea, but self-preservation kept me from giggling at the absurdity.

"If you must know, I'm a nature photographer. I was here trying to get photos of an endangered bird when your gun shots scared it off," I answered harshly, getting mad all over again at losing that shot.

"That doesn't tell me what you were doing here on *my* land."

I frowned. "Your land? This is a national park."

He shook his head. "No. The other side of the riverbed at the base of the mountain is National Park. Everything from there north for over five-hundred acres is my property," he corrected. I opened my mouth to argue and then stilled, somewhere in the back of my mind remembering seeing a private property sign. But it had appeared old and damaged and was on the ground. I thought someone must have dropped it or something.

"Oh."

The mountain of a man sighed heavily and shook his head. Well, other than being angry at having a random woman fall on him from a large height—and honestly, I could understand that—he hadn't shown any other signs that he was going to hurt me. Except his firm grip on the gun.

"Can you put that damned thing down? You're making me nervous," I grumbled, nodding to his gun.

"I scared away a pack of wolves when I took that shot. I'm not keen on putting down my gun anytime soon," he explained.

Again, oh.

He glowered at me a moment longer and I rolled my eyes and threw my hands up in the air in exasperation.

"Thank you," I mumbled.

"Sorry, what was that?" he asked as if he hadn't heard it. I glared and he cocked an eyebrow at me. Christ, that look made me want to smile. He was a huge man, an absolute giant with dark, slashing eyebrows, black hair and rugged beard which only added to his wild-man appearance. But that small eyebrow cock and spark of humor in his eyes did a lot to soften the image. Even if it was humor at my expense, and something told me that it was.

"I am not going to say it again," I said stubbornly, picking at the leaves on the ground. I swore I heard a gentle chuckle, but when I glanced up at him, he was facing the trees away from me and made some weird little whistle.

Silence stretched, and I watched as his eyes searched over me, as if he were trying to make his mind up about something.

"Putting aside the fact that you're out here on private property, why are you alone? And worse, why don't you have protection with you?"

"I *do* have protection with me. It's just… in my bag… beneath that bush," I answered, nodding toward the brush where my bag was sticking out.

"A lot of good it is going to do you over there."

I clenched my teeth. "I'm well-aware of that. Thanks, *Dad*."

He snickered and moved over to my belongings. I watched as he lifted it with no trouble at all, and I took a moment to appreciate the masculine picture he presented.

"Your dad should have taught you to never leave your weapon out of reach. More than that, he should have taught you never to go into unfamiliar woods alone," he muttered.

"You don't know my father, so you get to keep your opinions about what he should and should not have taught me to yourself," I snapped. He glanced up from my bag, blue eyes scanning my face with a strange amount of understanding before he nodded and glanced away. I brushed away the momentary rush of anger his words caused; he didn't know that my father had been my best friend, my protector, and my only parent. He didn't know that my dad had gone above and beyond to give me a great life, and he didn't know that my father was dead.

"Besides, he *did* teach me all those things. It was just a one-time slip that will *never* happen again," I added with feeling.

Mountain man nodded and looked behind him and then at me again.

"Can I approach you without you thinking I'm going to hurt you?" he asked.

"Are you going to let me have my bag and my gun?"

"Yes," he answered and hesitated. "Although I'd appreciate it if you kept your gun away with the safety on."

I opened my mouth to ask why, when a small girl strode confidently through the same path mountain man had, dressed in full camouflage. She wore a beanie over her head, but I could still see the bright red curls tucked up underneath it. Her wide blue eyes turned from her father, to me, and back again. She couldn't have been more than six.

"Where are you camped? We'll stick with you until we're sure you're not going to get eaten by wolves."

I glared. "Just so you know, you giant sasquatch, I've been doing this sort of thing my whole life, and I've never once been caught unawares before. This is a total anomaly," I assured, for some reason feeling the need to explain myself. I wasn't a city girl who decided I wanted a little wilderness and just walked into a random forest unprepared. I was an experienced hiker; I knew what I was doing.

Again, he raised that disbelieving eyebrow that made me grit my teeth.

"Sasquatch?"

"If the big foot fits."

"Mm-hmm."

Sighing, I turned my attention to the little girl and tried to give her a friendly smile.

"Hi, honey. Sorry if I scared you."

She grinned and shook her head. "Nope. My daddy will always keep me safe," she said with such confidence, my heart ached. God, I missed having that assurance, that protection and comfort. I smiled at her anyway, trying not to feel the heavy weight of my father's loss.

"I'm sure he would," I agreed.

"If you are worried about the wolves, why was your daughter alone?" I asked, turning back to her father.

"I hid her," he answered in a tone that told me he wasn't going to explain himself. I refrained from rolling my eyes—barely.

"You're really pretty," the girl complimented. I was momentarily struck silent and then ducked my head.

"Thank you, sweetheart. You're very pretty too, and you seem super brave to be out here in the woods."

She beamed at me and shrugged. "Daddy won't let me get hurt, and we're having a last a-ven-cha before I start school."

"Wow, it sounds like you guys have a great time planned. Sorry I'm putting a damper on it," I added, preparing to push myself to my feet.

"Do you like hiking?" she asked.

"I love it. I go all the time and have since I was about your age. My dad used to take me every chance we got," I explained, trying to get to my feet. Pain lanced up my leg again and I bit back a curse and fell back.

"Are you hurt?" mountain man asked, dropping his bag to the ground, and stepped closer.

"I twisted my ankle when I tried to get off you," I explained with a hiss of pain.

"Let me see," he demanded, and before I could protest, he carefully took my leg and rolled up the bottom of my pants.

"If you can just help me get upright, I'll be fine. I can make my way back to my camp on my own," I assured.

He grunted his acknowledgement, and this time, I did roll my eyes.

"Daddy says rolling your eyes is rude," the little girl told me. Mountain man turned to look at me with a raised eyebrow and I gave him my most innocent look before his beard twitched, indicating a small smile and he went back to inspecting my leg.

"It certainly can be seen as rude," I agreed.

"Do you like hunting?" the girl continued, shuffling close and sitting on the ground next to me. Mountain man paused and raised his head to look at his daughter, a small frown on his face. She beamed at him, and I heard him utter a small curse under his breath.

"Uh... I don't really like it. I know how to, and I understand when there is a need for it, but I love animals and I hate to kill them if I don't have to," I explained, wondering what that silent look had been about.

I looked the girl over a little closer. She was a very beautiful girl with eyes the same as her father's. Her hair was a dark red, a rare shade to see, and her skin was pale and porcelain. I hissed when the mountain man prodded at a particularly painful spot and my attention was drawn back to what he was doing. He grunted and pressed a few more places without taking my boot off.

"Ouch! That hurts, you Yeti!" I snapped.

"Yeti? Whatever happened to sasquatch?" he asked, turning to look at me with a small smile through his beard.

"I wanted to cover all my bases, I don't know what your kind like to be called," I returned hotly, willing myself not to cry like a baby. Damn, that hurt.

I hoped it wasn't broken.

"Well, think of another few creative words because I need to move your foot to see if you've broken anything," he warned.

"Oh great," I groaned and dropped my head back for a moment. Sucking in a deep breath, I nodded to him that I was ready, and he carefully began rotating my ankle. I bit my tongue and squeezed my eyes shut through the pain.

"Well, it doesn't seem like it's broken," mountain man finally said and stopped moving my foot. I let out a long exhale of air and let myself fall backwards onto the leaf-strewn ground, panting.

"Are you okay?" the little girl asked.

"Yeah, honey. I'll be fine, I just want to soak my foot in that stream a little to help with the swelling."

"I'm not sure taking your boot off is the right thing to do right now," mountain man piped up.

"Yeah, well… I have a bit of a trek to make it out of here, and I think the sooner I get something cold on my ankle, the better. I'd rather remove my shoe before they have to cut it off due to swelling," I retorted.

He considered this for a moment and then nodded.

"Okay, I'll help you over to the stream," he agreed. Smiling my thanks, I braced on one foot and extended my arm. He wrapped his hand around my forearm, and I was momentarily distracted by how big his hands were. Christ.

He gently pulled me up and it wasn't until I was standing in front of him that I realized how tall he was. I mean, I could tell from my tree that he was huge but standing right in front of him made me feel child-like.

I frowned and looked down at our feet to where I was balancing on one foot.

"What?" he asked, looking down as well.

"I was just looking to see if you were standing on a stump or something," I explained. Another flash of humor lit those blue eyes as well as a concealed smile behind his beard.

"Nope, you're just a shortcake."

I gasped in outrage. "I'm *not* short!"

He cocked an eyebrow and ran his eyes from my feet to my head and I didn't miss the flash of appreciation there. I glared and he swallowed a grin.

"What are you? Five-foot-two? That's short, ask anyone."

"I'm not five-foot-two," I snapped, tightening my hold on his arm so that I didn't topple over. He stared at me in disbelief, and I huffed. "I'm five-foot-three... there's a difference," I amended haughtily.

"Right, one whole inch. I'm sure it makes all the difference," he snickered.

"Well, according to you men, it does."

His eyes widened in surprise before he burst out laughing. I grinned and watched him laugh, struck with the oddest impression that he didn't do it often.

Wild man wrapped an arm around my waist so that I could lean against him, and we started moving towards the stream that was gushing water now. I was glad for all that rain we'd had a week ago, or this stream would only be a trickle. As it was, we'd have to be careful because I didn't want to slip and fall in. With how fast the water was running, I'd get swept away easily.

Wild man grabbed his bag as we moved closer to the water to get it out of our way.

"I love your hair. You're super pretty when you smile," the

little girl piped up behind us. I grinned and her father shook his head and muttered something under his breath.

"Uh… thanks, hon," I replied awkwardly.

"Do you know how to help my daddy so his junk doesn't fall off?" she asked.

I sputtered and turned quickly to look at her with shock.

"Mara!" Wild man shouted, letting me go as he spun quickly to look at his daughter, the momentum putting me off balance.

"Shit!" I gasped and fell backwards into him.

Chapter Three

SELINA

The bag flew from his grasp, and he wrapped his arms around me to stop me hitting the ground hard and we both went down. I rolled in time to see the bag wrench from his grip and tumble towards the riverbank, and I swore.

"The bag!"

"Shit!" he cursed and rolled out from beneath me to make a run for it. I watched as he made a last-ditch grab for it, but it was too fast. It hit the water with a loud splash, and wild man hurried for it, but the current was too strong. I struggled to my feet, using a tree branch to pull myself up in time to see the pack sink and disappear beneath the water.

"Fuck!" he roared.

"I'm so sorry," I gasped quickly, even though I wasn't sure I was totally to blame.

"I'm sorry too, Daddy," Mara added quietly, her blue eyes filling with tears.

Her father dropped his head back and closed his eyes, and I watched as he slowly dragged in several deep breaths. Mara slid up beside me and took my hand, her head hung low, her small sniffles breaking my heart.

"Hey now, sweetheart. This wasn't your fault," I tried to console, carefully kneeling in front of her. Big tears tracked down her face and she shook her head.

"Daddy said I wasn't allowed to use that word anymore, but I forgot," she whispered brokenly. I struggled to remember what she'd said and then bit my lip to stop from laughing. "Yeah, probably not a word a little girl should be using. Do you even know what it means?" I asked.

She shrugged. "My Uncle Jason told Daddy that he needed a girlfriend before his... *that word*... fell off. And I don't want my Daddy to fall apart because I like all of him and don't think any part of him is bad," she explained with such heartbreaking innocence. I bit my lip, but it was no good, the smile broke through anyway. Mara glanced at me, and I watched her lips tremble with a smile too.

I covered my mouth as a giggle worked its way up my throat and I tried hard not to laugh, but it was no use. Mara began to giggle too, and soon enough, we were both hunched over laughing. I have no idea what she thought was so funny, but my sides began to hurt.

"Are you done?" mountain man gritted out, but his despondent tone only made me crack up harder. Sometime later, I managed to drag in a full breath and hold back my laughter.

"I'm sorry," I apologized quietly, another quick giggle slipping.

"That bag had all our supplies, my SAT phone, our shelter and emergency supplies," he informed. Well, that did it. Any humor I had at the situation vanished and I ducked my head. Shit.

I watched him turn his attention to his daughter and she ducked her head again, crossing her little arms over her stomach. His expression softened noticeably, and he stalked forward until he came to kneel in front of her.

"I'm not mad at you, Mara, okay? No, you shouldn't have said that word, but it wasn't you who knocked me down," he comforted.

"Hey!" I gaped. He was *not* blaming this on me.

His eyes flashed with laughter when he looked back at me and then he turned to Mara once again.

"And it wasn't anyone's fault but mine that I let go of the bag. But we've talked about what happens in this situation, haven't we? So, what do we do?" he asked.

Mara straightened, and I watched as she thought hard.

"We don't have shelter. I have my water bottle, but you don't have yours. We don't have much food, only the energy bars you put in my bag," she listed off. "We still have your gun, but no more bullets," she went on slowly.

"And we have an injured person in our party. What do we do first?" he asked.

I smiled down at them and the way he handled her, the way he was teaching her. My heart clenched with memories of my father doing the same thing.

"We look after the injured person and see what needs to be done," Mara answered.

"That's right." Her father nodded and kissed her head. "We've already had a quick look, but we still need to get her ankle in the water, so let's deal with that first. We still have a good amount of daylight left, so we don't need to stress about shelter right now."

Mara nodded and smiled up at me and I grinned back.

"Let's try this again," mountain man said as he wrapped an arm around me once more.

"Thanks," I mumbled.

We took the last three steps to the riverbank in silence, and he carefully sat me on the edge and helped me to pull off my boot. I winced and the throbbing seemed to intensify. It was definitely swollen.

"You sprained it pretty good," he pointed out.

"Thanks for helping me. You didn't have to stay," I said quietly as he took a seat beside me and helped to lower my leg into the freezing mountain water. I inhaled sharply at the icy feel and closed my eyes for a moment. It hurt a lot, but the water would do it a world of good.

"I may be a sasquatch, as you call me, but I'm not going to leave an injured woman alone in the woods. Even if she is trespassing."

"Hey, you need to do something about your signs, then. You can't blame someone for coming out here when there are no clear signs," I defended, crossing my arms over my chest. His lips twitched as he watched my ankle, but he said nothing else. Mara came to sit beside her father on the other side and I closed my eyes, exhausted.

"Uh, I don't even know your name," I remembered.

He grinned. "Yeti isn't doing it for you?"

"Oh, it definitely suits you, but it's probably not polite to keep referring to you as such when you're helping me."

He smirked and shrugged.

"I didn't peg you for someone who believed in being polite, shortcake."

"Fine, stretch, don't tell me your name." I shrugged, sniffing indignantly.

"Stretch? Really? That's a name for a tall, lanky guy who can't grow a beard."

"Don't like it?" I asked with wide eyes. "Hmm, how about mountain man?"

He scoffed. "That's unoriginal since I am a man on a mountain."

"I've been referring to you as wild man in my head, will that do?"

"Again, not much creativity in that."

"Okay, fine. big guy?"

He shook his head.

"Ginormica?"

"Getting better," he assured.

"Gigantor?"

"What am I, a monster?"

I laughed and shook my head. "Okay, fine. How about Goliath?"

"Nah, David took down Goliath. I'm not that weak."

"Top-shelf?" I suggested.

He thought about that for a moment and shrugged. "It does make me sound like I'm the good stuff," he relented.

"Oh, you're right. That's a misleading name for you," I muttered. He pretended to look offended, and I sighed.

"Fine, BFG, but the F stands for fu—I mean... foolish," I stumbled, quickly amending my words when I remembered his daughter. He chuckled quietly and shook his head.

"Ooh, I know. Everest," I suggested.

He ran a hand over his beard and smirked before turning those electric blue eyes on me. "How about you call me Callan?"

Callan. Hmm, the name weirdly suited him.

"And you are?" he asked, raising an eyebrow.

"Oh no, my daddy taught me never to give my name to strangers," I teased. "Especially not ones who cost me the photo I'd trekked a week for and sat in a tree for hours in an uncomfortable position for."

"Ah, but by stopping to help you when you fell, you cost me and my daughter our supplies."

"You scared me with your wild, sasquatch appearance and made me stay in that tree longer than I should have, which caused me to fall in the first place, therefore injuring my ankle," I reminded. "Nope, you have to earn my name."

"Fine, in the meantime, I'll just call you shortcake," he agreed. I scoffed.

"No?" he asked and thought for a moment. "I'd say little lady, but the term *lady* doesn't seem to apply to you," he mused. I slapped him in the arm and tried not to wince. It was like hitting a brick wall.

He grinned and thought some more. "Smalls?"

"As in *you're killin' me?*"

"It's a great movie," he shrugged.

I shook my head.

"Peanut?"

I scrunched up my nose and he chuckled.

"Munchkin!" Mara suggested and I grinned.

"I do like that name," I agreed.

"It's what my Daddy sometimes calls me," she announced with a grin at her dad. Callan smiled warmly down at her, and my heart tugged again.

"My dad used to call me Buttercup and Darlin'," I explained, still able to hear his voice in my head.

"What does he call you now that you're a grown up?" Mara asked innocently. I glanced away from her for a moment and out to the running water before I shrugged and forced a smile I didn't feel.

"Nothing anymore. He died a while ago," I answered, trying not to let on how much it hurt that he was gone. I could still see him when I closed my eyes sometimes. He had been a big man like the neanderthal beside me, steady and strong and he seemed totally invincible. To see him in his final days was to see him as a shell of his former self, tired, sick, weak, and thin. I'd hated every moment of it, and yet I'd begged the universe for him to stay another day, another week. I knew it was selfish to ask, I knew he was in pain, but I'd only been seventeen, and the thought of losing my only family member, my father, my hero, left me feeling so frightened and alone. I shook my head to dispel the memory.

"That's sad," she said softly.

I nodded. "It is, but I have a lot of memories with him, and he was a good dad." I was desperate to change the subject because I had the most intense feeling that mountain man was watching me closely and that he caught a lot more about my feelings and thoughts than I wanted him to.

"What about little bit?" Callan offered, changing the subject. I smiled in appreciation and shook my head.

"That sounds like you're going to call me something else," I pointed out.

"Tater-tot?"

I laughed and shook my head.

"Squirt!" Mara suggested again with a giggle.

"Ankle-biter?" Callan added.

"What am I? Five?"

"You're almost as short as one," he returned.

"Nugget!" Mara giggled.

"Short Stuff?" Callan offered. Again, I shook my head with a grin.

"Half-pint?"

"I don't mind that one. It sounds fun." I laughed.

"Tinkerbell!" Mara shouted with excitement. I laughed and Callan wrapped his arm around her in a side-hug.

"Shortstop?" Callan suggested. I made a face and he grinned.

"Thumbelina!" Mara offered, looking cheeky.

"Oh, I know," Callan began and smirked at me. "Spitfire."

"That one makes me sound feisty, I like it," I agreed.

"Spitfire it is," he decided. I smiled and shook my head before dragging my gaze back to my ankle in the water.

"Or, you know, you can call me Selina," I said softly.

"Selina," Callan repeated softly, and I shivered at the way my name sounded rolling off his tongue.

We sat in silence a while longer, and it was only when my foot started to hurt from the cold that I took it out.

"We should probably put it back in the water every half an hour or so to help with the swelling," Callan said as he took another look at it.

"I have a first-aid kit in my bag with a compress we can put on it," I explained. Callan put my foot down gently and hurried to my bag, carefully sitting it a good couple of feet away from the stream. I told him where he could find it, and he came back a minute later.

"Okay, Mara. So, we're applying first aid to our injured party. What do we do now?" Callan asked his daughter.

"We still have some daytime left," Mara said, turning to look at the sun, raising her hand with four fingers pressed together. She was checking the time; this girl was incredible. "We should start trying to make our way home for a while before we get supplies for camp."

"That's right. And how do we find our way home?" he asked, carefully wrapping my ankle.

"To get to our home, I know we follow the stream uphill. But to get to town, we follow it down to the river and then follow the current," she answered confidently.

"Good girl. Okay, so Selina's ankle is wrapped up. How is your water looking?" he asked. Mara checked her water and showed him.

"Okay, so take a quick drink now and you need a refill, so very carefully fill your canteen, and put one of the purifying tablets in with it. Why aren't you going to drink from it straight away?" he asked.

"Because we need to wait at least half an hour for the tablet to work," Mara answered.

"So, look at your watch now, and then fill it up," Callan ordered. Mara took a good mouthful of her water and did as her father told her.

"If she has a watch, why was she checking the time with her fingers?" I asked.

Callan frowned at me as if it should have been obvious. "I'm teaching her survival skills. She could lose her watch, or it could break. If she can use the signs of nature around her, I'd prefer her to do that."

"That's amazing," I said in surprise.

Callan's lips hitched slightly in a smile, and he nodded. "I want her to be prepared. We live out in these woods, and if she ever gets lost and is on her own, I want her to know how to look after herself as well as I can prepare her."

"Well, you're doing an amazing job. Did your dad teach you too?" I asked, wincing as he tightened the bandage.

"No, ten years as a SEAL taught me wilderness survival," he answered. My eyes widened and I looked him over again. Of course. He had the build for it, that dangerous air and the ability to move in almost total silence despite the terrain and his size.

"Wow, that's impressive," I murmured.

"Your dad taught you?" he asked softly. I nodded and glanced at Mara who was screwing the lid back on her canteen and slipping it into her bag.

"My mother died before my first birthday, and it was just me and my dad until he died when I was seventeen. He never moved on from her, and he made me his entire life," I explained, realizing I was telling more than needed to be told, but I was trying to distract myself from the pain.

"He loved you." Callan made it a statement.

"I know he did. But I always felt guilty that he never moved on, never found someone else to love. I think he was too scared to bring someone else into our lives in case they were wrong for us," I explained. Callan tightened the strap and I gasped.

"Sorry," he said softly.

"Is that what you're doing with Mara? Protecting her from someone who might not be good enough?" I asked. Callan didn't answer for a moment, and I watched his jaw work.

"What makes you think that?"

"Mara is looking for a girlfriend for you. I have to assume it's because you're not dating anyone long-term."

Callan frowned and sighed with a small nod. "I loved Lina— my wife and Mara's mother. She died during childbirth... I was deployed when it happened."

I bit back my gasp and clenched my hands to stop from reaching out to comfort him. I got the impression it wouldn't be welcome.

"We were in the middle of an important mission at the time, and it was very tense. My superiors were informed Lina was in premature labor, but they didn't tell me, or they risked distracting me. I would have demanded to come home, but even if they had allowed it, they wouldn't have been able to get me back in time anyway, so they chose to say nothing," he continued, his voice low and deadly.

I kept silent. I understood his superior's decision, even if it sucked, but my heart broke for this man who no doubt went over every moment of that last mission and now knew that while he was doing that, his wife was dying, and his child was being born.

"I wish there was something I could say, Callan." I kept my

voice low, aware of Mara only a few feet away. He nodded and slid my sock back on over the bandage to help keep it warm while we traveled.

"Mara is my world," he stated, slowly raising his gaze to meet mine. "I stepped down from the teams immediately, finished my enlistment here on home soil and then left. She is everything to me, the last bit of my wife is in that little girl. I love her more than anything. She might be looking for a mother, but how do I begin to even trust another human being with her safety? Her heart?"

I didn't say anything for a moment and then slowly shook my head.

"I'm not a parent, so I can't offer you an opinion from that position, but you have to know, Callan, that you won't be able to protect her from everything in life. Someone will break her trust, someone else will break her heart, and she will learn how to deal with it based on the things you do."

"As her father, it's my job to limit the chances of that wherever possible," he began and then broke off, shaking his head. I watched him rub the back of his neck before he looked up at me, his eyes searching.

"Lately, Mara has made it known that she is shopping for a girlfriend for me and a potential mother for herself. But why would I bring a woman into our lives who could leave and break her heart? It seems selfish to try and date to improve my own happiness when the risk is damaging Mara's."

"This might not be my place to say anything, but I've never had much of a filter, and you seem like you could use some feminine advice while it's in your presence. Judging from everything you've said, I'm going to assume that doesn't happen often, so I'm just going to jump right in and say this now," I said quickly. Callan's eyes sparked with humor and his lips twitched beneath his beard, and he nodded his head once for me to continue.

"I understand you're scared to date and have the end result be that they walk out on you and that it will hurt Mara. But have you considered that you might find a woman who will love her like she's her own, raise her like she's her own, and give her a mother she apparently wants? I don't know the two of you all that well, but Mara seems easy to love, I don't doubt that when you're ready to date again, that whatever woman you allow yourself to fall in love with, will love her too," I comforted.

Callan's blue eyes swept over my face as he considered my words, and then he shook his head slightly.

"It's not something that's on the table right now anyway."

"But when it is—"

"Then I'll consider what you've said."

"Speaking as a daughter raised by her father," I interjected before he could stand up. He turned his attention back to me and waited. "I loved my dad. And I knew without a shadow of a doubt that he loved me and would protect me no matter what, but the one thing that hurt me the most was not seeing him happy like I'd seen other kids' parents. He did everything alone. I know he didn't mind, and it was just how life was for him... but it didn't have to be. He could have had someone to share his days with and look after him and bring us another kind of happiness we both missed out on," I explained softly, hoping I wasn't overstepping.

Callan took in my words, and I watched him consider them for a moment before he gave me a slight nod and climbed to his feet.

"Alright, Mara. What's next?" Callan asked his daughter, effectively ending our conversation.

"Now, we need to move before it starts to get dark," she announced proudly.

"That's right," he praised and stroked her head. Callan turned back to look at me and thought for a moment.

"I'm going to need to carry you."

"Oh, no. We can fashion me some kind of crutch," I suggested.

Callan shook his head. "We're going uphill, and we can't risk you falling again," he answered, putting the first aid kit back in my pack. He checked my water and put it back before making sure my gun was secure. He slung the strap of his rifle over his neck so that it rested between his shoulder-blades before he secured my pack to his back.

"You can't be serious," I muttered. "You can't carry me."

Callan knelt beside me and smiled, and up this close I could see the thick band of black that encircled his blue eyes, making them stand out that much more.

"Not only can I, but I will. We have a lot of ground to cover, and now that we're moving a little slower, we will have to spend the night out here. Mara and I are due home tomorrow at lunch. When we don't show up and no one can get a hold of us because my SAT phone is now sunk in the river, we're going to have five very worried SEAL's tracking us. I'd like to make it as easy as possible for them to do that."

I gaped, at a loss for words. He slid one arm around my back and the other under my thighs, and without even making a sound of struggle, he lifted me. I inhaled a sharp breath and quickly wrapped my arms around his neck to hold on.

If I hadn't been so flabbergasted, confused, and in pain, I probably would have swooned at his ability to carry not only my immensely heavy bag, but also me, with not even a grunt of effort.

"Alright, Half-pint, let's get going," he said softly to me. I laughed at the nickname and shook my head.

"Onwards, Top-Shelf."

"Come on, Mara, keep up, baby cakes," he called. For some reason, my heart did a little flutter at the way he called his daughter such an adorable name. His eyes flicked to me quickly and then away again.

"Stop looking at me like that."

"Like what?" I asked, a smile tugging at my lips.

"Like I'm... nice. Or soft."

"Why? Because you called your daughter *baby cakes*?" I asked with a raised eyebrow. I couldn't quite retain all my humor and I knew he could hear it in my voice.

"My daddy also calls me pumpkin, baby-girl, princess, and sweetheart," Mara piped up beside me. I glanced down at her innocent little face and back to her father who was gritting his teeth. I struggled to hide my smile and knew I'd failed when he glared at me again.

"Nope, I'm not looking at you in any particular way at all," I managed to say, but my voice wobbled with barely concealed laughter. His arms tightened around me for a moment, and he gave a low, deep growl. My breath hitched at the sound and all humor vanished in an instant.

That sound? The one that he made while his arms tightened around me had a heat coiling low inside me.

His eyes flickered back to my face and there was a glint in his eyes there, as if he *knew* the effect he'd just had on me. But that was crazy, right? He couldn't know. He stared at me for a few extra seconds, seconds that seemed to be filled with intrigue and want.

We walked in silence for a while, and I began to worry I was getting too heavy.

"Are you tired yet? You can put me down," I asked, focusing on his beard instead of his eyes. I like the beard. It was thick, but not overdone or wild. It was well-kept, but more than just stubble too. It looked good on him, adding to his mountain man appearance.

"I'm fine, you don't weigh much," he answered, a little frown on his face as if he disapproved.

"My weight is perfectly within the range for someone of my age and height," I replied, feeling defensive. He ran his eyes over me, running down my body slowly and then back up. My body tingled everywhere his gaze brushed and I refrained from doing something stupid, like tangling my fingers in his hair and tugging him closer for a kiss.

Damn, did I hit my head when I fell out of the tree?

Okay, I needed him to put me down soon because my wayward mind was stuck in a harlequin romance novel, and that just wasn't reality. I needed to remember this wasn't a rom-com movie, and strangers in the woods were usually dangerous. I was just lucky enough to have stumbled upon one who came equipped to scare off wolves and carry me to safety.

But he called his daughter baby cakes.

I inwardly groaned at myself. I was not going to be one of those women.

Callan adjusted his grip on me, his hand brushing my breast and I jumped and turned to him. His lips twitched under his beard and his eyes brightened slightly.

"Sorry," he mumbled. I glared, but the small smile trying to soften my lips ruined the effect.

"Sure you are," I muttered. His smile twitched again. "I don't mind if you need to stop," I offered. Because damn it, I needed to get away from him. I couldn't exactly class him as a stranger anymore, but it was so not okay for me to be having any tingly or heated thoughts and feelings about him.

"We need to cover more ground. Do you need to get down for a moment?" he asked. He was breathing a little heavier now, sweat beginning to wet his hair, but he didn't sound as if he was straining.

"If you need a break, I'm okay to stop," I offered. He nodded but said nothing else. I guess we weren't stopping yet then. I let out a small sigh at feeling like a damsel and faced ahead of us to the barely-there trail, beginning our journey back to the real world.

Chapter Four

CALLAN

The little spitfire was beginning to get heavy.

I knew she wasn't weighty in the least, but after carrying her and her pack for the last half an hour, I was beginning to strain.

I held the woman in my arms with ease and wondered where she'd come from and why I kept slipping into thoughts about us in my bed together. It wasn't like I had trouble finding female companionship. Whenever Mara went to visit her grandparents, I would find willing women happy to spend a night with me. I'd never taken them back to my home though. Firstly, it was usually too far from the bar I'd picked them up from. Secondly, it was my home, my sanctuary, a place for just me and Mara. I wasn't going to tarnish it with some random hook-up. So, what was it about this woman, this *stranger*, that had me envisioning her in *my* bed and *my* shower? Shit, I probably just needed to get laid. That was the problem. We continued the walk in much the same fashion. Neither of us spoke much more, and my thoughts were constantly see-sawing between lusty and confused.

I had kept up with a little of my SEAL training, so I knew I wasn't out of shape, but I wasn't up to par either when my arms began to burn faster than they would have had I still been an active SEAL.

Deciding I should put her down so that we could soak her ankle again, I called out to Mara to slow down.

"We need to soak your ankle again," I told Selina with a small huff. She nodded and braced on her other foot as I carefully set her down, and then she smiled up at me.

Well, fuck.

I had not been expecting to come across anyone today, much less a woman whose fiery eyes brought out a spark in me I thought long dead and a smile that had me waiting for the next one with bated breath. I wasn't a man who believed in pretty words or things like fate, but damn, I could write poems about her smile.

I slid the pack off my back and tugged her water bottle free of the side pocket. I took note of the kind of bag she had and was impressed. It was obvious that, despite the way I'd found her, she was an experienced hiker. Her bag was good quality, expensive, and well-used. From what little I could see on the outside, she had high-end equipment. Her clothes and hiking boots were made for comfort and camouflage, not these new trendy outfits I'd seen other hiker's wear.

She was the real deal which made me like her a whole lot more.

Her smart mouth, however… well, even that I didn't mind. "Alright baby girl, make sure you have a drink and a small rest. We'll get going again soon," I told Mara. She smiled up at me and I watched with a full heart as she sat down on the mossy ground by the stream and pulled out her own water bottle from her pack. I hadn't put much in it for now, just her water bottle, a spare jacket, some energy bars, and a compass. She wore a watch with a GPS built into it just in case we somehow got separated; I wanted to be able to find her at all times. I was also teaching her how to use a compass in case she did get lost. She knew to head home if that happened. So, we'd been training with that today, and I wanted her to get used to carrying her own things. Being only six, I didn't want to overload her.

When we left the house two days ago, I'd locked up and left a letter for Jason and the crew. They all knew we were going camping, and I'd left instructions on where I'd planned for us to go. I was nothing if not prepared to get lost or for something to go wrong. Well... I had *thought* I was prepared. I hadn't anticipated a drop-dead gorgeous woman falling out of a tree and into my lap.

Literally.

I planned to be back home tomorrow by lunch, but judging by how little ground we'd been able to cover in the last half an hour, I knew we were going to be late. Glancing up at the sky, I frowned. I didn't like how dark those clouds were getting either, or the small breeze that had started to pick up. When I'd checked the weather for our trip, we were supposed to get rain a day after we got back home; but it looked like the bad weather had moved faster than anticipated. At least I knew my team would come looking and that it wouldn't be hard to get moving once they did. Mara could only walk so far and so fast, and I could only carry Selina for short amounts of time. I had kept up with my training, sure, but it was going to get harder and harder to carry her the longer I had to do it. But I *would* do it. Even if it rained, I'd carry her out of here because there was no other option.

I'd spotted the fresh wolf tracks earlier this morning and was keeping an eye out for any more signs of them. They were all through these woods, as were bears and other predators, and mostly I didn't mind living in peace with them. But I wasn't stupid, either. I knew when to go off course to avoid a pack of wolves because we were too close to their den, or a mama bear with her cubs, but when I realized the wolves were tracking back, I began to get concerned that they had decided to hunt me and Mara. Mostly, wolves avoid humans, especially when there is other game to hunt, but their behavior had been off, and I was concerned we were on the menu. After hiding Mara in a high tree with the instruction that she was not to come down unless I gave our signal—the whistle—I'd gone looking for them. I had seen them, crouched low in the brush and had been on alert. I wondered why they were sitting there, as if they were staking out their prey. I'd seen no evidence of a den nearby, but my alarms had been blaring that something was wrong.

Not wanting to take a chance, I'd shot off a couple of rounds, knowing the loud sounds would scare them off. After making sure they were truly gone I'd started to head back to Mara and found that backpack. Seeing Selina up in the tree, it all suddenly clicked why the wolves were circling. They'd spotted their prey and were waiting for her to climb down from her spot.

My blood ran cold now at the thought of what could have happened had we not been out there. Would she have reached her gun in time to scare them off? Or would she have met a painful fate at their teeth?

Wolves and bears were here all the time, and if someone wasn't prepared, they easily became lunch for a hungry predator.

I shook my head now and took several mouthfuls of her water bottle before I handed the rest to her. Selina accepted the bottle with a small smile and took a drink before she got to work unwrapping her ankle.

She'd been prepared, but none of her equipment had been on her. A stupid move, and I knew she thought so too. It was obvious that her anger and frustration was at herself for leaving her rifle too far out of reach.

Then we started talking and all that sass and attitude came out, and I'd wanted to poke at her some more just to see how riled she got. Maybe I still would. A sick part of me liked watching that fire flare in her eyes whenever she thought I was being backwards or an asshole. And I was, but I was also smart. Being out here in these woods, especially alone, was not for the faint of heart, and if you were stupid, then you got dead fast. She had almost been a meal for a pack of wolves, only I wasn't sure she realized it.

I studied Selina now as she carefully took care of her injury. She was small, but not tiny. Her curves were all woman, and I noticed right away. When she'd first crossed her arms over her stomach, all indignant and pouty, it had pushed her breasts together and up and I was only human; it was hard not to notice. I was pretty sure she'd caught me too, but she hadn't called me out on it. And the way she felt in my arms... She was soft where a woman should be soft, but she was toned too. Usually, I liked my women with a little more meat on their bones, something to hold onto when I fucked them... but the strength in her small body told me that she had stamina, and that made for interesting thoughts of all-night rounds of hot, sweaty sex. She had those intense brown eyes to match her dark hair, eyes that were hooded and secretive. The phrase *bedroom eyes* came to mind, and I finally knew what that meant. And that hair? It was tied back in a braid, but it was long and thick, the kind of hair I could already feel trailing over my thighs as her hot breath neared my aching cock. The kind of hair I could wrap in a fist and hold onto as I took her from behind—

"Hey!" She snapped her fingers at me, and I blinked. Her cheeks were pink again and she was sitting with her legs and arms crossed, her expression telling me that she knew *exactly* what I had been thinking.

I grinned, unable to hide the smile and her eyes dipped to my mouth. Some of the anger vanished to be replaced by something else entirely. Hmm... looks like I wasn't the only one thinking steamy thoughts. She had been affected earlier when I'd growled at her, I knew she had. I'd felt her swift intake of breath and her eyes had gone hazy, lustful. I was trained to pick up on small nuances in people, and I could see a woman's interest in me a mile away. Call me a cocky bastard if you wanted, but I wasn't about to pretend I didn't know. Turning to check on Mara, I watched her sitting with her legs crossed as she carefully closed the lid on her bottle. A small smile tugged at my lips as she tucked her bottle away again and checked the laces on her shoes. I'd taught her to check them often, I didn't want her to trip and hurt herself.

"You guys must hike often," Selina observed, watching Mara and me.

I shrugged. "We hunt for what we need, and we camp when we feel like it."

With another quick smile, Selina edged slowly to the stream and lowered her foot into the running water. She hissed and I watched her grit her teeth and then slowly relax. My gaze returned to the water, and I wanted to curse again. All our things had been in that bag. Our shelter, our food, first-aid, SAT phone, literally everything we needed. I couldn't believe it had gone in the water. I flicked another look at Mara and ran a hand over my beard, wiping away my smile. That little hellfire sure knew how to leave me speechless. Fuck, she *had* to stop asking people to help me stop *my junk falling off*. Fucking Jason and Cohen; I was going to smack both of those morons when I saw them tomorrow. They really had to watch what they said around my little girl. She was a sponge and picked up everything. My mind returned to my conversation with Selina about her father never moving on and I frowned. As much as the thought weighed on me, it was good to hear from a woman who had grown up without a mother and whose father had never moved on. She was giving me an understanding of how life would be for Mara. Sure, she seemed to have turned out well enough. She was confident, witty, and intelligent, but she was also... lonely. I recognized it in her because I saw it in myself. Yes, I loved my daughter with all my heart, and *nothing* would convince me to bring a woman into her life if I thought she would abandon her and leave us heartbroken, but what if Selina was right? What if Mara was suffering because she could pick up on my loneliness? To know that you were the reason your parent never moved on had to be a heavy burden, and I could see that it bothered Selina to know her father never knew that kind of love again because he didn't want to risk anyone damaging his girl.

I was doing the same thing with Mara.

Shaking my head, I sighed. I wasn't ready to move on yet anyway. One-night stands were it for me, but maybe it was worth considering at some point... trying to move on?

My gaze traveled back to Selina as she sat on the riverbank beside my daughter who was happily chatting away about what she thought school would be like and how much she was looking forward to it. To move on, she'd have to be one spectacular woman. Lina had been my wife, and I'd loved her like nothing else.

Selina was instructing Mara to gather some long-stemmed white flowers nearby, and I watched curiously from my seat on a log. Mara brought over a bundle of them, and Selina, still keeping her foot in the icy water, began twisting them and bending them. Mara watched with rapt attention and then gasped in delight.

Selina had turned the flowers into a crown.

"There, a crown for a princess," Selina said, putting the flowers on Mara's head. My heart clenched as Mara's face glowed with happiness and she spun to look at me, her bright blue eyes luminous, her red hair fanning out around her.

"Daddy, look!" she cried, leaping up to run at me. I caught her without question and lifted her up into my arms.

"That is awesome," I agreed.

"I'm a *real* princess now, Daddy!" she cried. I smiled and kissed her soft cheek.

"No matter what, you'll always be a princess to me, baby-girl."

She beamed at me and wiggled her little legs until I let her go, and I watched her run back to Selina who was watching us with an expression of part heartbreak, part adoration.

I could understand that look, and it didn't sit right with me that she'd suffered such loss in her life. I wished there was something I could do to help her, but I knew very well there wasn't.

"Thank you, Selina, for my crown," Mara said bashfully before she leaned forward to hug her. Selina's eyes widened briefly before she beamed and hugged her back. The look on her face was one I could understand completely; my daughter was damn easy to love.

After a moment of watching them talk, the hair on the back of my neck stood up and I stiffened slightly, taking a slow, careful look around us. Suddenly, I couldn't shake the feeling that we were being watched. I'd say I was getting paranoid, but I had a sixth sense about these kinds of things, and I'd never been wrong before.

Were we being stalked by a predator again, or something altogether different?

I listened as Mara and Selina talked and laughed. Selina asked her a heap of questions and kept up the same level of enthusiasm without talking down to her. What people didn't seem to grasp about Mara was that she was actually pretty intelligent, but Selina never spoke to her as if she couldn't understand.

I watched the two of them, but my senses were flared, trying to figure out where the danger was coming from. But nothing stood out.

"Alright, it's getting late. We should get going," I reminded. Selina nodded and pulled her foot out of the river. I moved closer and carefully lifted her before putting her on the log I'd just been sitting on. I dried her foot as best I could before wrapping it again.

"Mara, take a small drink, baby, and put your water away," I instructed, moving a little faster. That feeling was increasing, and I couldn't shake the sense that something was about to go wrong.

Mara nodded and dragged her backpack closer to us, her little eyes flicking around us for a moment. Did she sense it too? Every protective instinct I had screamed at me to get my daughter and Selina out of here before something bad happened.

Selina put her hand to her chest and froze, her face paling and eyes widening.

"Selina?"

She glanced down, checked down her shirt and then looked around her wildly.

"Selina, what's wrong?"

"My necklace," she gasped, distress printed clearly on her face. "I lost my necklace."

"Okay… well, why don't we get home, and when your ankle is better, we can come back?" I suggested, but she was already shaking her head.

"No, no, I can't leave without that necklace," she pleaded.

"What's so important—"

"It has my father's ashes in it," she cut me off, her voice thick with emotion. My eyes widened and I shook my head.

"Shit."

"I can't leave here without that necklace, Callan. I can't, it's all I have of him," she pleaded. I grumbled and rubbed the back of my neck, that nagging feeling that we were being watched still there. The last thing I wanted to do was trek further into the woods to get a damned necklace. But it wasn't just any necklace…

"Look, you guys go," Selina told me, struggling to her feet. "I'll go back for my necklace and find you when I have it," she suggested.

"No," I ground out.

"Callan, I'm not making you two go back with me, you have Mara to think about. But I can't leave here without getting that necklace. I won't," she told me, her face full of determination, her dark eyes filled with pain.

Fuck.

"I can't let you go back alone," I muttered. Her eyes shone with unshed tears, and she shook her head.

"I have already made your day awful; I don't want to add to it. Just give me my water canteen, and you can take my pack with you and find somewhere to set up camp. It has my shelter in it and anything else you might need for the night. You can get Mara settled in, and I won't be far. I'll take my rifle," she explained, hobbling around me and grasping a tree trunk.

"And how do you intend to get back up the mountainside? Going down without slipping and further injuring yourself will be hard enough. How are you going to get back up?" I demanded.

"I'll figure something out, I always do." She shrugged, starting to limp away.

"Selina," I sighed, running a tired hand over my face.

"Go, Callan. It's only half an hour back. I'll find my necklace, soak my ankle for ten minutes and then come back. With my ankle the way it is, I'll be three hours, tops," she assured.

"And by then it will be dark, and wolves will come out hunting," I reminded her. Not to mention I felt like there was something else hunting us, but I didn't want to tell her that yet.

"I have my rifle," she pointed out, leaning down to tug it free of her pack.

For fuck's sake!

I strode towards her quickly and yanked the rifle from her hands. Selina spun on one foot to look at me, her eyes wide and lips parted. She wobbled slightly and gripped the front of my shirt for balance, and I placed my other hand on her lower back to help steady her.

A beat of silence passed between us, and I was once again possessed with that insane urge to kiss her senseless. Her gaze grew unfocussed and slipped down to my mouth, and it took actual effort not to groan and follow through with my desires. As it was, I pressed her closer with my hand and gripped the rifle tighter in the other.

"You aren't going anywhere alone," I ground out instead. She blinked quickly and her focus moved back to my eyes.

"Callan," she started with a small frown, shaking her head.

"Like you said, it's only half an hour back. I can get you down the hill faster than if you try it yourself, and I can get you back up faster too," I explained.

"But Mara—"

"Mara loves hiking and will be fine. We'll rest if we need to, but I'm not letting you walk off injured, alone, with night approaching, and wolves in the area," I explained, watching her long lashes as they lowered and then lifted again, her expression uncertain.

"I wouldn't go back if I didn't have to." Her eyes were full of guilt and sorrow, but I understood her inability to leave it behind. I nodded, my hand on her back gentling, fingers stroking.

"I know, and I get it," I replied softly.

Neither of us spoke for a moment, and I found myself leaning into her, feeling that ache in my body intensify and my thoughts drift to places it shouldn't.

"All ready, Daddy!" Mara called happily.

My daughter's voice was enough to jolt us out of whatever daze we'd been in, and I stepped back carefully, making sure Selina was stable before I reluctantly let her go. She ducked her head, and I cleared my throat, looking back up at the sky.

"Alright, let's hurry. I don't like the look of that sky, and I'd like to have some kind of shelter sorted in case it turns nasty," I announced quickly, checking Mara over to make sure she had everything and to give myself something to do other than look at Selina who was becoming more and more tempting.

"Are we going to find your necklace, Selina?" Mara asked kindly.

"If you don't mind going back with me," she answered.

"Nope, that's okay," Mara agreed happily before skipping

ahead. I watched her drag her beanie back over the flower crown and over her long red hair and then bent to pick up the pack. I secured the rifle back to it and then turned to the woman I was quickly wanting to hold in my arms all the time.

"Are you ready?" I asked.

Selina studied me for a long moment and then nodded. She raised an arm and put it around my neck, and I lifted her into my arms.

"Callan?"

I glanced down at her and she was looking at me with warm, soft brown eyes.

"Yes?"

"Thank you," she whispered. I squeezed her gently in response and she smiled and laid her head on my shoulder. Sucking in a steadying breath, I kept a wary eye out as we started carefully back down the mountain to where I'd found Selina in the tree.

Chapter Five

CALLAN

We'd been walking for about fifteen minutes, and my neck was itching with the feeling of being watched. Fuck, if I were on my own, I'd have no problem calling out whoever it was to get this showdown over with, but I had Mara and Selina to think about.

I wasn't sure who was following us or why, but I didn't have a good feeling about it. Worse, I didn't think they'd wait too long before making themselves known, and I wasn't sure what to expect. We had two rifles for protection, but I wasn't sure how many bullets Selina had brought with her, and all of my supplies had been washed down the stream.

I glanced around us again, hoping to catch some sign of who was hanging around, but nothing stood out.

"Everything okay?" Selina asked softly, her voice lowered so Mara wouldn't overhear. I glanced back at her, and as had become a habit, my eyes slid to her soft looking mouth and back to her beautiful brown eyes before I replied.

"You'll think I'm crazy," I answered, my voice a little strained from effort.

"No, I won't. You have a look on your face right now. I know I've never seen you in action before, but I feel like I'm looking at your soldier face," she answered with a small smile, but her eyes were serious and full of concern. She was picking up on my alarm and it worried her.

I shook my head and dropped my voice so we wouldn't be

overheard. "I think we're being followed—watched. I can feel it. I don't know if it's an animal or…" I trailed off, not wanting to scare her.

"Or a person," she added softly, paling slightly.

"It could be nothing," I said quickly, rushing to reassure her.

"But you don't think so." She made it a statement. I hesitated in answering and she slid her other hand up my chest to get my attention. I dragged my eyes back to hers and she frowned gently.

"I like to be prepared, and I can't do that if you're not being honest. I can take it, whatever the truth is. So don't lie to me to save my feelings. I'm not prone to hysterics, and I can handle a situation better if I can see it coming," she told me softly.

I let out a slow breath and nodded, my respect for her rising. "I don't think I'm mistaken. I feel like we're being followed."

"You don't think it's one of your friends a day early?" she asked.

I shook my head. "No. My guys wouldn't play with me like that. It wouldn't end well for them, and they know it."

Selina swallowed hard, and I watched the brief flash of fear in her eyes as she looked past us to Mara. When her gaze came back to rest on me, it was with steely resolve.

"I could be overreacting in my predictions of how this is going to end, but I'm a girl who needs a *Just in Case Plan*… so, if it comes down to having to run for safety, then you put me down, you pick up Mara, and you run." The protest was there on my lips, and she clenched my shirt in her fist.

"Your daughter is your world, and I won't have you hesitate because your sense of duty is tested. I know that given the choice, you'll save your daughter over a practical stranger anyway, no matter how much it pained you to leave me behind, but I wanted to voice it so that you know if it comes down to it, you're not abandoning me, you're saving your daughter and being a good father. We're the adults, and so our concern must be for Mara's safety above each other's. I'll do what I can on my own, but I want you to know that I *want* you to protect her and get her to safety. I won't beg you to save me," she insisted softly.

I frowned at her, trying to read that look on her face, the tone in her voice. Saving Mara would be my priority absolutely, but it doesn't mean I wouldn't hesitate in what to do when the safety of another innocent was at stake. I couldn't imagine dropping Selina to run my daughter to safety, but no one else was here to do it, and, if push came to shove, my daughter came first. It sucked having the scenario laid out for me, but she wasn't wrong. My respect for her rose again, which made the whole thing that much harder.

"*If* it comes down to it, *if*... then I get Mara to safety. But then I'm coming back for you. You do what you have to do to stay safe, and I'll come back for you," I assured her. Her lips tilted up at the corners, but her eyes were tired and serious. What was that look?

"Is there something more going on, Selina?"

She shook her head, and when she blinked again, that bone-deep weariness in her eyes was gone. I knew she was lying, I could see it, feel it... but I wasn't sure she'd tell me even if I kept asking.

We continued on in silence, Mara leading the way as I called out directions to her. She'd picked up her left and right quickly, and she was holding her compass, attempting to use it to direct us. The feeling of being watched didn't disappear, but I could see no signs of anyone else anywhere.

I adjusted my hold on Selina, and she let herself relax into me.

I glanced down at her to see her gnawing on her lower lip. Her eyes drifted to my face and stopped, heat stealing up her cheeks. I watched in fascination as her already dark eyes turned liquid, and I dropped my gaze to her lips. Who would have thought that it took a woman literally landing in my lap for me to be so tempted?

We reached the clearing in record time. Going downhill was riskier when carrying an injured person, but I was able to use the momentum to keep up a steady pace, and

Mara didn't have any problems keeping up. My arms and back were aching by the time we got to the clearing, however, and I was grateful to be able to put Selina down without needing a break earlier and delaying us further.

In the last half an hour, the wind had picked up and the clouds darkened further. We were about to be hit with a storm, and I wanted to get to some cover before that happened. My eyes darted to Mara who was happily chatting away about her toys at home and my gut clenched. I needed to keep her safe.

"What does your necklace look like?" I asked Selina as I carefully put her down. She hopped on one foot to the tree and placed her hand on it to keep steady.

"It is a gold chain with a pendant on it that looks almost like a little canteen. It's not very big, maybe the size of a quarter," she answered, searching the ground around her. Mara got down on the ground and started pushing away leaves and I joined her. Selina's distress was increasing with every moment, and so I moved to the stream to see if it was anywhere near there. Ten minutes went by with no luck, and I glanced at Selina who seemed like she was about to start crying.

Shit.

I ran a hand over my hair, my senses still screaming at me that we were being watched. The sky was darker again, and I could hear the faint rumblings of thunder in the distance. My eyes caught on the tree she'd fallen out of, and I frowned. Edging closer, I looked again and then sighed in relief.

"Found it!" I called.

"Where?" Selina gasped. I pointed up into the tree where it hung, glinting in the fading and dulled sun.

"Oh my God," she cried, looking like she was on the verge of tears. I made my way over to the tree and carefully climbed it. Once there, I unhooked it from where it was caught on a twig and took a quick look around the forest from this vantage point. The storm was coming from the south, and by the looks of those clouds, it was going to be a decent one.

"We need to find some shelter," I called down to them before I dropped out of the tree, landing carefully. I handed Selina the necklace, frowning at the little golden flower on it

"You didn't say it had another charm," I noted. Selina took the chain and frowned.

"It doesn't," she answered and peered down at it. I watched as she froze, and the color in her face drained away. She swayed slightly and put a hand out to steady herself against the tree trunk, her eyes glued to the necklace.

"Selina?" I called, stepping in close, my alarms blaring now. She took the flower charm between two fingers and worked it off the chain before she tossed it out into the forest, her gaze skittering around us like she was looking for something.

Or someone.

My gut clenched, and I remembered the fear on her face when I'd mentioned we were being followed by a person. She knew who it was.

I glanced at Mara and stepped in close to Selina.

"You need to tell me who is following us, and why."

She looked up at me, her wide eyes filled with fear and remorse. "I-I'm sorry, Callan. I didn't know... I didn't mean for you two to get caught up in this," she apologized, her tear-filled eyes searching around us fearfully.

"Selina—" I started, but a giant boom of thunder above us drowned out the rest. She gasped and Mara ran over to me, her wide blue eyes frightened.

"We need to get to cover," I called over the wind that suddenly picked up. Selina nodded and put the chain around her neck again before giving Mara a reassuring smile. I watched a moment longer, and the look on her face was one of uncertainty. Whether she was worried about the storm or the fucker following us, I wasn't sure. Probably a combination of both. I climbed back into the tree and looked around. There had to be somewhere nearby we could hide.

After another massive boom of thunder and lightning striking in the distance, I caught sight of a group of boulders on the other side of the stream. It wasn't ideal, but it was close and better than nothing. I hurried down and picked up Selina.

"Come on, Mara," I called. She stuck to my side as I hurried us to the stream. It was running too fast for me to walk us across. I searched up and down it, but there was nowhere narrow enough for us to jump across.

"Wait here," I told them as I carefully put Selina down. "Do you have a hatchet?" I asked Selina, sliding her pack off my back.

"Yes," she answered and hurriedly pulled it out.

"I'm going to make us a bridge, we have to be quick. There are a set of boulders across the river just there. You see them?" I asked, pointing. Selina nodded. "I'll get us over there. As soon as we're there, we need to collect as much wood as we can before we get soaked. I'll do that while you secure the area and give us some shelter," I informed her. Selina nodded again, her lips set in a thin line of determination, her dark eyes sharp and intelligent while they continued to scan the area around us. I was bursting to know what she knew, but we didn't have time right now. At the very least, I appreciated that she wasn't panicking or going to pieces on me.

"Stay with Selina while I do this, okay, Mara? Don't leave her side," I leaned down to tell my daughter. Her wide blue eyes were filled with fear, but she nodded and reached out to take Selina's hand who was quick to pull her close and offer her words of comfort.

Without wasting any more time, I hurried to one of the trees by the stream that wasn't too wide, but still wide enough for us to walk on without it snapping. It would be risky, but it was the only way. I didn't want us caught out in this storm. I swung the hatchet and prayed it wouldn't break as I got to work cutting down the tree. I should have known better— Selina didn't buy dodgy equipment. The hatchet was strong and sharp, and made quick work of the tree. It fell as I'd hoped, right across the stream. Selina and Mara came slowly over to me, Selina hopping.

"I'm going to test it first, then I'll come back," I called over the wind.

They nodded and I wasted no time in going across. It was a little perilous, the tree bounced under my weight, and it was hard to keep my balance with the rushing water beneath it and the strong wind, but it didn't snap, and I knew if I hurried, I'd get us all across safe. I secured the pack on my back and quickly moved back to them, I held my arms out for Mara. It was going to be easier to take the weight of the pack with Mara then it would be with Selina. I wasn't sure the tree was going to hold up well under both our weight as it was, and I didn't want to test it with the added pounds of hiking gear. "Come on, baby. I am going to take you across first," I told her. Mara looked worried and I smiled assuredly.

"It's okay, princess. You know I won't let anything happen to you." She nodded and I brushed a kiss over her cheek as I lifted her into my arms.

"I'll be right back. Don't move," I told Selina. She nodded, but her eyes were worried as she watched us go. My mind tried to imagine if this was that moment we'd talked about, and I had to take Mara and run. I took another look at Selina standing there, injured, beautiful, worried… I couldn't imagine leaving her behind. Having to do it in a dangerous situation would haunt me. I only hoped my team found us before that became necessary.

Turning back to the task at hand, I told Mara to wrap her arms around me and hold on tight and to close her eyes. The last thing I needed was her panicking and trying to climb up higher and throw me off balance. The tree trunk was only wide enough for me to put one foot directly in front of the other. Any slip, and we'd end up in the stream.

Carefully, but as quickly as I could manage, I walked us across the tree trunk. As I stepped onto the other side, it began to lightly rain. Shit. We were running out of time. I placed Mara on the ground and tossed the pack down beside her.

"Wait here, baby, I'll be right back," I assured her. She nodded and I kissed her head quickly and left. She was so tiny standing there in the darkening forest, watching me with wide, blue eyes. Fuck, I hated this.

I almost jogged across the trunk and swept Selina up without pause. She drew in a sharp breath, and I jogged us over to the riverbank.

"I'm going to get you to climb onto my back so I can see where I'm putting my feet. Once you're there, try not to move or lean in any direction," I told her. Selina nodded and I adjusted her so that she could climb onto my back. She wrapped her legs and arms around me, and for a split second, a part of me wished we were doing this with her on my front... alone... naked.

Banishing the thought, I stepped close to the trunk and drew in a steadying breath. For a moment, I imagined falling from the trunk and Selina and I getting swept away. My gaze snapped to Mara standing on the other side and I clenched my jaw. No. It wasn't going to happen because I couldn't afford for it to happen. Mara would be out here, all alone, and I refused to think of anything bad happening to her.

"Ready?" I called to Selina as the rain began to pick up.

"Yes!" she shouted and buried her face in my back. I sucked in a breath and started across the trunk. The timber beneath my feet bowed slightly and I inwardly cursed but kept my cool. I had to hurry; I wasn't sure this would last much longer. Selina's grip on me tightened ever so slightly, but she remained otherwise still, solid, refusing to move an inch. I gripped her legs around my waist tighter and kept going, one foot in front of the other, my gaze focused on the bank on the opposite side and not the tree beneath my feet. The water was making me dizzy, and I wanted to see what I was aiming for. *Almost there...*

The wind picked up suddenly and slammed into us. I wobbled precariously, throwing out my arms to keep us balanced. Mara cried out for us, and Selina gripped me tightly, her sharp inhale loud by my ear. I kept us upright and moved forward another couple of steps, gritting my teeth.

When my foot landed on the shore on the opposite side, I

almost collapsed in relief. Selina slid from my back quickly and Mara hurried over. I caught her as she threw herself at me and I wrapped up her tiny trembling body.

"We're okay," I comforted, holding her tightly. "Let's get some shelter, okay, baby?" I told her. She nodded but didn't loosen her grip on me.

"Mara, we're okay," I reassured, kissing her cheek. She slowly pulled away from me, and her blue eyes were filled with tears. I kissed her again and put her on her feet before I threw the pack on my back and swept Selina up. We were on the move before she had properly wrapped her arms around me, but I wanted us out of this storm and somewhere dry immediately.

The sun should still be up for another hour, but with the storm coming in, we were losing visibility fast. We made it to the set of boulders, and I sent out a silent thank you to the universe. They were piled on top of each other so that the boulders were stacked and there was about fifteen feet by twelve feet space beneath them.

It wasn't much, but it was better than nothing. I tugged Mara inside and dropped the pack beside her.

"Okay, Mara. I want you to use your hands and dig out a little fire-pit in the middle here. Leave enough room around it so we can all sit around it. Do you remember how to do it?" I asked, having shown her only twice before. I didn't really need a fire pit, but I wanted to distract her, to keep her busy so she wouldn't be consumed with fear. She nodded, but her face was pale and drawn.

"Hey, I need you to do this, okay, princess? I am going to get firewood, and Selina will stay right here with you," I comforted. We were running out of time to do this, but I couldn't just leave her there when she looked so frightened.

"Okay," she whispered. I watched her go and turned to Selina. "I've got her. You grab what you can and come back," she told me, her dark eyes promising me that she would look after Mara. I nodded, scooped up the hatchet and got to work. I wasn't far away from them, and hurriedly cut branches down. The rain was beginning to pick up, and I needed to get as much dry wood as possible.

I grabbed an armful of wood and dropped it at the entrance to our shelter before I ran out to get more. By the time I came back the third time, we had a good pile of timber, Selina had a fire going and was setting up some blankets towards the back of the cave to make a bed.

I went out for one last run, determined for us to have enough to last the night. The rain was coming down hard now, and I knew it was pointless to stay out any longer. By the time I got back inside, I was soaked. Selina, too, was wet and I wondered why but then I saw the fallen tree branches she had dragged over to the entrance of the cave to try and provide us with some kind of windbreak.

"Are we sleeping here tonight, Daddy?" Mara asked, and I was glad to see she was dry.

"Sure are, pumpkin," I said and sank with a heavy breath onto the leaf strewn ground. I was exhausted, wet, and hungry.

I took in the small fire Selina had started and noted the collapsible stand over it. I frowned and was about to ask what she was doing when she shuffled backwards and grabbed a small tin kettle in the corner. She had created a funnel out of leaves and had filled it up.

"I have instant meals in my pack, so we only need to add hot water to them and we're good to go. They're actually really good," she explained. I smiled in appreciation and took a moment to simply breathe. It was nice to have someone else around who thought of these things. I wondered if that's what it would be like if I ever dated someone seriously. Would they be a true partner? Could I let them take some of the responsibility, or had I grown too used to taking charge that I'd drive them away?

Selina hooked the small kettle onto the collapsible stand and the kettle hung over the open fire to boil. Working with Selina made it feel easy to do. Would it be the same with someone else?

I turned to Mara who had taken off her beanie and shoes and smiled.

"How are you doing, munchkin?"

"The bridge was scary," she whispered.

"You were really brave, Mara," Selina praised. Mara nodded slowly, but still looked at me.

"You were, baby cakes. Very brave," I added.

We sat in silence for a little while as I thought about everything that had happened since this morning. I'd known this woman for only a few hours, but already I felt like I knew her better than most people. We clicked, somehow. Had it only been around lunch that she'd fallen from the tree and onto me? Shaking my head, I ran my hand through my wet hair.

I started talking to Mara about what we'd done over the last two days, trying to take her mind off the storm raging around us and her memory of the stream. Soon enough, she was back to her usual animated self and had Selina laughing about some of our hiking trips together. Selina shared some of her stories about her and her dad, and I was impressed at the trips she'd taken at such a young age. I wanted to take Mara to the Grand Canyon and walk all the way down to the bottom. I'd only ever seen it once before, and we didn't hike into it.

Selina pulled out the meals in a packet and we each sat in silence as we ate. I was grateful that we hadn't lost her pack and that she had enough food for all of us. It was warm, which was amazing, and tasted far better than I thought possible. When we were done, I wrapped Mara in the sleeping bag and within two minutes, she was fast asleep.

Sighing, I turned back to look at Selina and grimaced. "We need to talk."

Chapter Six

CALLAN

Selina's wide dark eyes were solemn, and she nodded slowly. She shivered and I frowned, remembering we were both still wet from the downpour. I took a quick look at the dark forest around us; it was still raining, but thankfully the wind was coming from the other direction, and we weren't being flooded. The occasional flash of lightning lit up the sky, but by the sounds of the thunder, the storm was passing over.

"You need to get dry first," I told Selina when she shivered again.

She shook her head, her face averted, and I frowned. I opened my mouth to tell her she didn't need to get sick on top of being injured, but then caught sight of the pink on her cheeks and bit back a smile. She was shy, and we had nowhere else for her to change but here.

"I can be an adult about it if you can," I offered. She choked on a small laugh and glanced back up at me, brown eyes shining.

"What about you? You don't have anything dry to wear."

I shrugged. "That's no reason for you to stay in wet clothes. Do you need help, or can you manage on your own?" I asked. Half of me hoped she needed help while the other half pleaded that she could do it alone. This woman was tempting enough, I didn't need images of her half-naked in my head to make it worse.

"I think I can manage," she mumbled, rifling through her bag. I tried to ignore the disappointment that snagged at me, and nodded.

"I'll be over here," I said, pointing to Mara. I could keep my back to her, but that was all the privacy I could give.

I watched my little girl sleep and wished today hadn't been so scary for her. She was so little, lying there under the blankets, her beautiful porcelain face just reinforcing to me how fragile she actually was.

I tried desperately to ignore the sounds of clothing being removed and tried even harder not to close my eyes and picture what Selina might look like. It was several minutes later when she cursed softly under her breath and exhaled impatiently.

"Everything okay?" I asked.

"I, uh... I think I'm going to need some help."

Swallowing hard, I turned around to face her and inwardly groaned. Nothing could have prepared me for the sight of her in a tank top, sans bra, and her pants loosened and half-way down her thighs.

"I can't keep my balance and pull them off. And I can't put pressure on my right foot and kick them off," she explained. My eyes were glued to the little strip of bare skin visible between the elastic waistband of her underwear and the hem of her gray top. For some reason, it was an incredibly erotic sight.

"Hey!" she snapped. I dragged my eyes back to her face and she was trying not to laugh. "You're being an adult about this, remember?"

"Yep," I bit out. I was thinking *very* adult thoughts about her. Not wanting to make her uncomfortable, I took the two steps required to be at her side and helped her to sit back down. Clearing my throat, I leaned over her, trying my hardest not to stare at her hardened nipples beneath the cotton shirt.

Fuck, she was beautiful.

Slowly, I grabbed the waistband of her pants and began pulling them down her long legs. Inches of golden tanned skin were revealed, and my eyes drank in every part of it. I was desperately trying to be clinical about it, but it was impossible.

I heard her breath catch as I pulled the material to her knees and paused. Her dark eyes were liquid heat, and I felt my body react predictably.

"You need to spread your knees," I instructed, my voice rough. I was sure she could read how much I wanted her, but considering I could see the same kind of hunger in her eyes, I didn't try to conceal it.

Slowly, Selina parted her legs, and I closed my eyes for a moment, struggling not to look elsewhere.

Again, I continued dragging her pants down, my fingers grazing smooth skin, and one by one, slowly pulled them off her feet, being particularly careful with her right foot.

As soon as the pants were gone, we both breathed out audibly and I glanced back at her. Her face was burning pink and she dropped her gaze before handing me a pair of thermal leggings.

Once again, I got to work sliding them over her feet, a part of me hating to cover up all that skin, but it was for the best… for a lot of reasons. I helped her to stand and balance against the wall as I remained on my knees and dragged the material up over her backside, my fingers brushing her skin. She inhaled sharply and I paused for a moment, my gaze dipping once again to that tantalizing strip of bare flesh.

"There," I mumbled when she was covered.

"Thank you," she whispered and after another couple of seconds, I edged away from her. I took a moment to get myself under control as she pulled on a thick shirt and jacket. I shuffled to the other side of the fire and sat close, hoping to dry off a little during the night.

When she was finally fully dressed, I reached out and tugged on her leg, and she let me pull her ankle onto my lap to look at it.

"The swelling looks to have gone down a little," I commented, checking it carefully for signs of further injury.

"It doesn't ache quite as much," she offered. I nodded and gently stroked the skin of her foot. She stilled, but didn't try to pull away. After a long pause, I turned to stare back to her. She ran a hand through her brown hair, now loose and long down her back.

"My dad died when I was seventeen. I'd already finished school and I had a job, so I petitioned the courts to stay out of foster care. My request was granted, and I started traveling around, trying to find a place that felt like home," she began, looking off into the low flames.

"Four years later, I met a guy, Patterson, and I thought I'd found home. We got on really well, and he was amazing, protective, and intelligent. He challenged me, never let me give up on anything and pushed me to be more. He worked as a professional hacker, and big companies would pay him to test their internet security and help them fix it," she continued.

I made sure not to interrupt her as I waited for her to find the right words.

"He was an intense man, in every aspect. At first, I loved that about him. He was forceful about my safety and took it seriously, wanting to know where I was all the time so he could look out for me. He always wanted to look after me. He was intense about his job and could get lost in it for a day without so much as stopping for a break. He was passionate, and I thought that was amazing. He was even..." She trailed off, her cheeks warming again, and she looked uncomfortable. "What?" I asked softly. She swallowed hard and kept her gaze averted from mine.

"He was quite intense in bed too. It made things interesting, passionate, and exhilarating... until it wasn't," she added, ducking her head. My stomach began to cramp at the total note of dispassion and pain in the tail-end of that comment.

"I was barely twenty-one, and my whole life I'd only ever had one man who loved me so deeply. Then when he died, I was mostly alone, and I had no real friends, so I didn't spot the red flags before it was too late," she added and then sighed heavily and pushed on. "He started being forceful in bed, and it scared me... he liked to cause pain. But I was far more scared to say no or to leave than I was to fight him on it. It was like he knew my every move and thought before I did, and he had a reason ready for everything, so I felt crazy and like I was overreacting. Until he did it again and I was yet again too scared to move on," she continued, her tone filled with weariness.

Her voice was small, her eyes averted, and body held stiff as she recounted her past. I wanted to say something to comfort her, but she wasn't done yet.

"Every time he realized he pushed me too far, he'd go out and buy me a flower charm for a bracelet he brought me months before." I remembered the flower charm she'd yanked off her necklace and my concern increased.

"I tried to leave not long after, but my bank accounts were wiped clean. They didn't even exist. He was the only one I knew who was that good, but I couldn't prove it. I still left, but everywhere I went, I had problems. Job offers fell through, creditors were looking for me, my car was found to be unregistered when I *knew* I'd only recently registered it. I knew it was him, and it took forever to get someone to believe me enough to investigate it," she continued.

"Did they help?"

She shrugged. "They agreed that it was suspicious and that it looked like I had a problem. They recommended a name change and a move. I agreed and left. That was three years ago. Every now and then, he finds me again, he tracks me down, and things start going wrong in my life," she added, turning her head to look out into the rainy night.

I didn't even think of her age, she was only twenty-four, still so young. I immediately felt like a brute for thinking steamy thoughts about her. Yes, she was twenty-four and well into her adult years, but I was thirty-five and had a kid, eleven years was a bit of an age-gap. I watched her now, the way she was still trying to find words.

"There's more, isn't there?" I asked and she nodded. When she turned back to look at me, it was with wide, haunted eyes. "He started escalating by trashing my apartment and vandalizing my car. He would stalk me, take photos, and post them around my room when I was out. I had a cat once... and he..." she trailed off, her voice turning rough, and her face filled with disgust. "He skinned it and left it on my table," she finished in a rush.

Disgust and alarm rolled through me.

"I didn't risk buying more animals after that, but I looked after a neighbor's dog another time, and he killed it... tortured it first by breaking its legs and jaw," she added, closing her eyes as a tear escaped.

"And now he's found you again."

"I am so sorry, Callan. I didn't know he'd found me again, or I never would have let you and Mara help me," she said quickly, her chocolate eyes brimming with tears.

Fuck.

This guy was a nut, and he had escalated to violence. If he was out there in the forest now, waiting and watching for us, and I had to assume it *was* him that was watching us, then we were in trouble. I refrained from looking at Mara, my worry for her safety compounding with every piece of information Selina divulged.

"How can he track us like he has been? I'm a SEAL, it shouldn't be that hard for me to find him."

The reluctance on her face had my worry increasing. "He was an operative once, but he got kicked out. He said it was all bureaucratic stuff, but I think they saw that he was unhinged," Selina explained.

Fuck!

I ran a hand over my face and exhaled heavily. We were stuck in the woods with an injured party and an ex-team's guy who had gone off the rails and had started hunting his ex.

"I'm so sorry," she repeated.

I ran a hand over my head and shook it.

"It's not your fault, Selina. You didn't do this." I wasn't mad at her, but I was mad at the situation. Fuck... hell of a week to go camping. Although, if we hadn't come, then who knows what would have happened to Selina. Would the wolves have gotten to her, or would it have been her ex?

Neither option was comforting.

The rain continued to pour down outside, and I wondered if it would let up in the morning. We needed to leave early, but I didn't want Mara to have to walk in the rain, I didn't want to risk her getting sick. The wet ground would be harder to traverse going uphill, especially carrying Selina. Her ankle may be improving, but it hasn't healed yet and I didn't want to increase the damage by letting her walk.

From the corner of my eye, I saw Selina shiver slightly and I hated that she was cold. I grabbed the pack and put it behind me so that I could lay out but remained sitting up slightly and then turned to look at her.

"Come here," I said, tilting my head. She frowned and I raised an arm for her to duck under.

"It's cold and you gave my daughter your blanket so she'd be warm. You can sleep beside me, and we'll keep each other warm. I'll just use your other jacket as a barrier so you don't have to lie against my damp clothes," I told her, indicating the sleeve poking out of her bag.

"Oh, no, th-that's okay," she stuttered.

"So, you'll let me freeze tonight, half-pint?" I asked, knowing her compassion wouldn't allow me to go cold.

"What happened to spitfire?"

I shrugged. "I'll alternate your names."

She gave a low laugh and peeked at me from beneath her lashes as she bit her lower lip indecisively. *Fuck me*, that look.

"Come on, I'm getting cold," I urged, trying not to pay attention to how much I wanted to hold her.

"You're sure?"

"At the very least, it's survival 101 to share body heat."

"And at the most?" she asked with a cocked eyebrow.

"At the most, I'm trying to cop a feel without being obvious."

A startled laugh escaped her, and I grinned, loving that look on her face. With a small shake of her head and a sigh of resignation, Selina adjusted herself and scooted over to me. I placed the jacket along my side where she'd lay and gently wrapped an arm around her shoulders to pull her tight against me. Shit, she felt so good to hold.

"Is this okay?" she asked softly, holding herself stiff, uncertain. I reached down and grabbed her under one of her knees and pulled it half up over my body before dragging her arm across my chest, so she was wrapped around me. Her small sound of surprise was music to my ears.

"Now it is."

I didn't need to see her to know she was blushing, but I looked anyway, a grin tugging at my lips as she continued to gnaw on her lip. I slowly raised my hand and pulled her lip from between her teeth, and I felt her sharp inhale. The feel of her hot breath on my fingers caused a stirring in my pants and she slowly tipped her head back to look at me.

"You're going to make your lip bleed," I explained softly, my eyes were trapped in her gaze, all chocolate brown, burning amber in the firelight. Her long lashes swept downwards as she once again focused on my mouth. Her leg tightened on me, and I bit back a groan at feeling her soft curves pressed into me.

I froze when she shifted up slightly, her face in line with mine, her sleek hair sliding over her shoulder. Heart hammering, breath trapped in my lungs, I watched as she slowly lowered her face, and her lips brushed my cheek gently. Throbbing started down low, and I hoped like hell she didn't notice it.

"Thank you, Callan, for everything." Her voice was a whisper of sound as she hovered over me, her lips *so damn close*. I recognized the look of hunger in her eyes for what it was and inwardly cursed. There was a moment of tense, crackling silence where the possibility of more hung between us. I swallowed hard, my body screaming at me to wrap my arms around her and pull her down, to devour her mouth and bunch my hands in that silky mahogany hair. I wanted to slide my hands up her slim waist, beneath her shirt and cup those breasts pressing hard against me.

"Go to sleep, Selina. I'll take the first watch." I barely refrained from swooping in and kissing her senseless. Another silence where she seemed to weigh my words against the tension between us. Her smile was small and understanding and she pulled back slightly.

"Are you sure you don't want me to go on the first watch?" I nodded, and she smiled gently in appreciation before lowering her head back down to my chest. She tucked herself in tight against me and I held her close, closing my eyes to breathe her in.

It took a long time for my body to unlock and relax beneath her. Only then was I sure I wouldn't pounce on her and take what my body and mind were urging me to take.

I had no idea what it was about this woman that called to me, that drew me in and made me want to throw caution to the wind, but whatever it was, it was fucking strong, and I wasn't sure I was ready to explore it.

It was something I could think about later, though, because first we had to get home safely.

Chapter Seven

SELINA

It took Callan a long time to finally fall asleep when it was my turn to keep watch. I'd listened to his even breathing, his steady heartbeat, and soaked in the feeling of safety in his arms. It was crazy how safe this man made me feel when I'd known him less than twenty-four hours. But in that time, we'd been through so much, shared so much. The way I felt when we were together, it was as if I'd known him for years, it was so effortless.

I wanted to stay here where I felt safe and cared for, but safety in the arms of another was an illusion I wouldn't let myself fall for again. The only person who had ever been capable of providing that for me was my father, and he was dead.

My mind returned to the issue that plagued me throughout the night.

Patterson.

When we'd gotten together, he'd been larger than life, overwhelming. He was a lot to take in all at once, and being so much, it was beyond amazing to be caught up in his stare, in his attention. He was incredibly intelligent, so being able to captivate a man like that had felt like nothing else. But all along, there had been something lurking beneath the surface, something I hadn't realized was sick and twisted before it was too late.

Patterson liked to hurt people, it's what really turned him on. And I wasn't talking about a BDSM kink where both partners were willing and had signals and clear lines in the sand. No, Patterson liked it when his partner was in actual pain, and the more they screamed, the more he wanted it, the harder he fucked, the more intense his obsession. He was a sadist, a *true* sadist. From what I knew after some research, true sadists like Patterson were pretty rare. I was lucky that the damage he'd inflicted on me had been minimal at the time. He liked to draw long, thin lines on my body with a sharp blade, so delicate that they didn't scar, but they hurt so much. Patterson had learned the art of causing pain that would not show lasting damage. He was an artist in his own right, and no one, *no one,* left him.

I blinked as I glanced over at Callan and Mara, and my heart clenched.

I had to leave them.

Patterson was relentless, and he was jealous. I'd tried dating twice after I left him. The first guy had come home to find his entire house trashed, lounges and carpets slashed, rubbish everywhere, and a message in spray paint on the wall that said *leave her alone.* The second guy had come home to find a dead rabbit nailed to his door with the same note.

I made it a point not to date anymore.

I was worried that seeing me with Callan would trigger Patterson's jealous streak, and that he would target him like he'd targeted the others even though Callan and I weren't dating. What worried me more, was that Patterson was likely to pick up on the fact that Callan was a military man. He always had been able to point out an ex-military man, or one still enlisted. He would know Callan couldn't be scared off with a dead animal or a trashed house… so what would he do? My gaze tracked back to Mara and my stomach coiled tight in denial. I couldn't let that sweet little girl get hurt because she and her father had been in the wrong spot at the wrong time. Callan had been asleep for a few hours now, and the sky was beginning to lighter. I was supposed to have woken him an hour or so ago, but he needed his strength, and I needed to get away from him and his daughter. Carefully, I lifted myself off Callan and silently pushed to my feet, biting my lip when my ankle screamed at me. It was not healed, but at least it wasn't as bad as yesterday. I could hobble my way out of here, somewhere far enough away that I could lead Patterson from them. I looked around and frowned. I'd take my water canteen because Callan and Mara could share hers, and I'd take my rifle. I didn't hold out much hope that I could take Patterson out, but I wasn't going out there without some form of protection. I was sacrificing myself, sure, but I wasn't going down without a fight.

I wasn't going with him, period.

When I had my supplies, I moved as quietly as possible to the entrance and paused. I glanced over my shoulder one last time and wished I could stay, wished I could get to know them more. For some inexplicable reason, I felt like I was meant to find these two. But maybe we were too late now. Wishing I could cuddle Mara one last time, wishing I could have time to explore the chemistry between myself and Callan, I mouthed a silent goodbye and hobbled out of the cave, using the rifle in my hand as a temporary crutch. I was thankful the sky was brighter now, but it still took a little time to get up the small rise beside the cave. At least it was easier than I had been anticipating. Once up there, I slung the rifle over my shoulder, slid the canteen strap over my neck and used the cave as a wall to lean against. There was a tree only twenty feet away; I could use a branch from there as a crutch to help me get out of here faster.

"Where do you think you're going?"

I spun around quickly at Callan's growling voice and gripped the side of the boulder for support. I forgot how tall he was.

"Uh…" I trailed off, unable to come up with a convincing lie in the face of all his glowering fury.

"I know you're not sneaking off to try to lead your lunatic ex-boyfriend away from us," he snapped.

"Callan—"

"Because I know you're not that stupid," he hissed.

"I just—"

"Just what?" he interrupted. "You're injured, Selina. He'll find you, which I guess is what you want because you have this insane idea that you're sacrificing yourself for us so that Mara and I don't become targets," Callan began angrily.

"Well… yes."

"No."

"I don't want you and Mara mixed up in all of this," I tried to explain, adjusting the rifle strap on my shoulder.

"We're already in this."

"If I go now, then you guys will be safe," I pointed out.

"And what do I tell Mara when she wakes up? From what you've told me, the guy is unhinged. What happens if he decides he's mad at you and hurts you, and out here in these echoing hills, we have to listen to you screaming? What happens if he decides he's had enough, and kills you, and we come across your dead body?" Callan continued, stalking forward until I was backed against the boulder.

"I don't think—" I began, but Callan yanked the rifle from my shoulder and tossed it onto the ground, doing the same with my canteen around my neck before he caged me in with a strong arm on either side of my head.

"What happens when you're gone, and I want to see you

again? What happens when I can't find you, and I'm never able to sleep because I'm still looking for you, worried about you?" he continued softly, his face mere inches from mine and set in hard lines of anger and something else... something a lot hotter.

Oh, wow.

"I just want to protect you and Mara," I defended softly, my body waking up at his closeness.

"Mara is mine to protect, and I will do it when it becomes necessary. Until then, we have help on the way today, and I'm not letting you out of my sight for a second before it becomes absolutely necessary. Got it?" he ground out, his blue eyes blazing at me. He lowered his head slightly and I parted my lips, my body screaming for attention, my mind short-circuiting.

"Tell me you understand, Selina," he said softly. I licked my lips and he groaned, his eyes locked on my mouth.

"I-I understand," I murmured. A slow, satisfied smile curled his lips.

"That's my girl," he whispered. My whole body combusted with those words, and he closed the gap between us, crushing his lips to mine. I gasped, and his tongue slipped into my mouth, his lips sealing us together in a heated, passionate kiss. Sliding my hands up his chest, I bunched his shirt in my hands as he pressed himself against me so that I could feel every part of him. The heat from his body seeped into mine, the feel of his strength left me feeling like putty in his hands. I moaned into his mouth, kissing him back, sliding my hands over his broad shoulders to sink into his thick hair. I tugged gently and he growled against my mouth, his hands sliding down my sides, raking sparks and zaps along my body, to my thighs where he lifted me effortlessly. I wrapped my legs around his waist, my ankle twinging but I ignored it when he ground himself against me.

I cried out against his mouth, and he kissed down my jaw to my neck where he nipped and then soothed with a raspy swipe of his tongue. His hands slid up my waist again, beneath my shirt to cup my breast through my thin bra. My head lulled back, and I moaned low as he plucked at my hardened nipples and ground himself against me again, groaning as I rolled my hips with him, rocking, willing him to do it again.

"Callan," I whimpered, wishing we were both naked and somewhere we could take our time.

"We have to stop," he warned, his voice a low growl, and I could tell it was with obvious effort that he stopped grinding his hips. He was throbbing between my legs and his breathing was as uneven as mine. I dragged my gaze back to his face and his blue eyes were burning, as bright as the hottest flame. He slowly lowered my feet back to the ground, but he didn't back up, keeping us pressed tightly together. I stared up at him, my body weeping at the thought of putting an end to this, but my brain knew it was the right thing to do. Callan cupped my cheek and swiped his thumb back and forth.

"No more trying to leave us."

A tiny part of me I tried to squash immediately read way too far into those words, heard them loud and clear and wished he was saying he didn't want me to leave them *ever*. I erased the thought immediately and nodded slowly. Callan's lips curved softly and lowered his face back to mine, and I tipped my head back to kiss him.

This kiss was a lot slower, gentler, more exploratory and less dominating. I couldn't decide which I liked best, because the man sure knew how to kiss a woman senseless. On and on it seemed to go, his hands on my waist, above my clothes this time, his body still pinning me to the boulder as he took his time.

I had absolutely no complaints, not until—

"Daddy, is Selina going to be your girlfriend now?"

We pulled apart like we'd been burned, and I gasped, looking down at Mara who stood by the cave entrance, her long red curls cascading down her back and her big blue eyes wide with curiosity.

"Mara," Callan said her name quickly, running a hand over his hair.

"'Cause if you get a girlfriend, then I get a mommy. And Selina is all the things you said were good for a mommy to have," Mara continued on as if seeing her father kissing a woman like he needed her the way he needed air wasn't strange.

"No... Mara, it's not—" Callan tried to explain but she talked over him.

"You said a good mommy for me had to be smart and like hiking and like nature and had to be pretty and nice. Selina is all those things," she concluded happily, planting her little hands on her hips like she was waiting for an answer.

An awkward silence descended, and I bit my lip to stop from laughing at Callan's stunned expression and utter speechlessness.

"Uh, hey, Mara. We have to get going, honey. Do you think you can help me pack up our stuff?" I asked.

"Are you my dad's girlfriend?" she asked, tipping her head back to look at me inquisitively.

"Uh... no, honey. And I know that must be confusing for you, but maybe you can talk to your dad about it when you're back home?" I suggested. Mara sighed and dropped her hands.

"Fine," she sulked before she turned and headed back for the cave. I turned to look at Callan who was still staring at the spot Mara had been in, his eyes wide and hand frozen in his hair.

"Hey, papa bear?" I called, clicking my fingers at him to break into his thoughts. He blinked and turned to me, and I grinned. "Can you grab the rifle and the canteen?" I asked.

"Uh… yeah," Callan mumbled, shaking off his shock. With another grin, I carefully followed Mara into the cave, my mood for the day brightening.

~

"Is your daddy really in your necklace?" Mara asked several hours later when we stopped for a rest.

Callan had been carving a "W" into a tree at every stop starting at the cave, and when I'd asked him what he was doing, he said that his team would definitely be looking for them right now, and that a lot of our previous tracks would have been washed away by the rain. He needed to leave them a sign that they'd been here on the off-chance they came this way. When I asked him why a "W", he said it was because his call-sign was Wolf. I liked that… Wolf. He most certainly was an alpha.

We'd been walking since before sun-up, and it was a little after noon. Twice we'd stopped to soak my ankle in the stream again and the swelling had gone down noticeably.

"Uh, yes," I stammered, not sure how to have this conversation with a six-year-old. Did she understand what cremation was, or would it horrify her?

"That's cool," she said as she chewed on the energy bar, her blue eyes on the necklace. "My Mommy isn't in a necklace, she's everywhere."

"Oh," I said awkwardly. I wanted to ask questions, but I didn't know how. Mara nodded easily and finished what was in her mouth.

"Daddy says that everyone is made up of good stuff and bad stuff. But not Mommy. Mommy was made up of *only* good stuff, and she had *so* much of it that the universe needed to take her back so that there was enough good stuff to spread all over the world. Now, whenever someone does something nice or good, I know that it's a part of my mommy that made them do it," she explained easily.

My heart turned over at that and I flicked a quick glance at Callan whose eyes were glued to his daughter. His gaze strayed to me, and I sent him a reassuring smile. He was doing such an amazing job raising his daughter, I wasn't even sure he knew it.

"Your whole dad isn't in there though, is he?" she asked, pointing to my necklace.

"No, sweetheart, just a little bit so I can take him with me everywhere," I answered kindly. She nodded and smiled.

"I think your daddy is out there too, like my mommy, and they're spreading good stuff everywhere," she mused innocently. If I didn't love this little girl before, I did now. She was so innocent, so pure... so good.

"You know... I think you got a lot of your mom's goodness," I told her. Mara's face broke into a huge grin.

"Really?"

"Absolutely," I answered quickly. She smiled and finished her power bar before tucking the rubbish back into her pack. I was glad she understood to do that, but I shouldn't have expected any less when she had Callan as a father.

I turned back to the man in question, but his face was unreadable as he stared at me. I wanted to know what he was thinking, but at the same time, I wasn't sure it was a good idea.

"We should get going again. We have some more ground to cover, and unless someone finds us soon, we'll be camping again tonight. I'd like time to put together a decent shelter," Callan announced. I nodded and looked down at Mara.

"You ready, honey?" I asked.

"Yep."

I'd never met a kid so happy to walk in all my life. But Mara was all about nature, and she never got tired of her surroundings.

Chapter Eight

SELINA

It had been a long day, but Callan finally agreed it was time to set up camp. I told him about my one-person shelter in my bag that had been useless last night, and we agreed to set that up for Mara and that the two of us would be fine under the stars.

Callan stepped away to start collecting firewood, and I stayed with Mara who helped me to put up the shelter and roll out the sleeping bag.

We were all tired, hungry, and sweaty. The drenching we'd copped last night had helped a little with our smell, but after today's trek, all of us were getting a little on the ripe side.

Once the firewood was collected, Callan took Mara down to the stream to help her wash off, especially since this part of the river was less likely to sweep us away.

I made the fire and got everything set up so that when Callan came back with the kettle, we could start boiling water. We were low on food, and so Callan and I agreed to make sure Mara ate, but we were rationing what was left, which meant half an energy bar each was our dinner. We were only another six to eight hours walk from his house apparently, but we wanted to be prepared in case something went wrong, like my ex making an appearance.

We hadn't seen him today, and Callan hadn't mentioned feeling like we were being watched again, but I was still uneasy. There was no mistaking he had been out here with us, that flower charm had been proof enough.

A few minutes later, Callan came up the river holding Mara in one arm, who was dressed in my second to last clean shirt and the kettle in the other hand. All their clothes had been in their pack, so I was happy to share what I could. My heart did a strange little flutter at the sight of this big, military man smiling at his little girl, saying something that made her giggle. God, my ovaries just clenched.

Once Callan had Mara settled in the shelter by the fire, I carefully stood up. After resting it last night, I could walk small distances, and it was a good thing too, because I hadn't wanted to rely on Callan to walk me somewhere so I could pee.

"I'm going to go down to the river to wash off," I told him. He paused and glanced at me and then to the water.

"I don't like you being out of my sight," he explained.

"I know, but it's not really appropriate for you to be there with me, the same for Mara, and we can't leave her alone," I replied, picking up my rifle.

Callan grimaced. "Can you wait? I know you must really want to get clean, but it doesn't feel worth it," he asked.

"I'll be fine," I assured. "I'll be ten minutes at most, and I'll call out if anything is wrong. Plus, I have my rifle," I reminded, bending down to pick up the washcloth and soap I'd packed and allowed Mara to use.

"You can't have your gun in the water, which means it will be out of your hands, which means there is a possibility you won't get to it in time if you need it," he explained, his brows turning downward.

"I'm going," I told him, moving carefully. "I won't be long," I added and stepped away. I felt Callan's eyes on me until I walked stiffly out of sight, and I breathed out heavily. I didn't want to be away from them any longer than necessary either, but bathing was becoming less of a desire and more of a need. With a quick look around, I placed the rifle on the ground and kicked off my shoes and socks as quickly as I could with my sore ankle before stripping. I didn't give myself time to think about how cold the water was, I just limped in, gasping as it hit sensitive skin. Just as quickly, I dunked my head under the water and scrubbed at my scalp with my fingers, desperate to lift away the sweat and dirt that had accumulated there.

When I broke the surface again, I inhaled sharply but grinned. Damn, it felt good to get clean. I moved to the shore and grabbed the soap and washcloth and got to work cleaning myself. Once that was done, I dragged my clothes into the water and scrubbed them. The only reason I was doing this was because I had one spare sleep shirt left in my bag, and it came down to my knees. It had the faded words *World's Best Dad* on it, and it used to be my father's. It had stopped smelling of him a long time ago, but it was a comfort item I took with me whenever I went hiking. It was the first Father's Day gift I'd ever been able to buy him with my own money, and he'd worn it so much it was a little worn. So, I'd be in wet clothes for a few minutes until I changed; it was worth it.

When I finished washing my clothes, I squeezed them out as best I could and laid them on the flat rock bed beside me and then took a moment to simply appreciate the beautiful sunset before me. I was chilly, yes, but I was clean and felt alive and the view before me was breathtaking.

"Beautiful view," a voice called. I spun and ducked, lowering my body until only my head stuck out of the water.

A man stood on the bank a few feet away, dressed in full hiking gear. If I hadn't been so stressed about being naked, I would have been able to appreciate his stunning looks more.

As it was, I was still momentarily sidetracked by his gunmetal gray eyes and sandy blonde hair, wide shoulders and tall stature.

"Sorry, I didn't mean to frighten you, but there's really no polite way to approach someone bathing naked in a river," he called, staying a few feet away. My gaze drifted to my rifle on the shore, and he caught sight of it too.

"I don't mean any harm, seriously. I'm sorry for scaring you," he added.

"Can I help you?" I demanded, keeping my arms crossed over my chest.

"I hope so," he answered, raking a hand over his head. Something about him was familiar. Not as if I'd seen him before, but in the way he stood, the air about him. "I'm looking for someone who has gone missing," he answered. My breath caught and hope sparked. Was this one of Callan's teammates? That would explain why the look of him was familiar.

"Description?" I asked.

"Male, thirty-five years old, six-foot-four, black hair and beard, blue eyes. He would have been with a six-year-old girl, dark red hair, and blue eyes. They were supposed to be home this afternoon. We tried calling his SAT phone yesterday to warn him of the storm, but he never replied and that's not like him. We're all worried," he explained.

Relief slammed into me, and I took a moment to scrub a hand over my face.

"Which one are you? Cohen or Jason?" I asked.

Surprise colored his face and he smiled. "Cohen," he answered. "I take it you've met them?" he asked.

I nodded and grinned. "Yes, they helped me yesterday when I injured my ankle, we've been together ever since. They're just over the ridge," I explained.

Relief was evident on his face, and he slumped forward, bracing his hands on his knees.

"Oh, thank Christ. The storm rolled in faster than anyone predicted, and when he didn't answer the phone, we were all worried. Wait, why didn't he answer?" Cohen asked. I shivered and he held out a hand. "Sorry, why don't you get out and get dry first, you must be freezing," he cut in, looking at the fading sun. His eyes tracked to my wet clothes, and he frowned.

"Do you have anything dry?" he asked.

"Back at the camp."

"Here," he began and pulled his pack off before rifling through it. He held out a long-sleeved shirt, big enough that it would be like a dress. "You can wear this that way you don't have to wear wet clothes back up there."

"Oh... uh... thanks," I gaped, having not expected it.

"Can I come closer?" he asked. I nodded, but still watched him cautiously. He came up to the water's edge and placed the shirt by my wet clothes, his eyes lingering on me a little longer than they should.

"I'd appreciate you at least *pretending* to be a gentleman and turning around while I dress," I told him, my cheeks burning. Cohen chuckled and held up his hands in surrender and turned his back. It was a pleasant sound, and I noticed that he had dimples. Sheesh, this man probably reeled all the ladies in.

"So, talk to me. What happened?" Cohen asked, his back still turned.

I started with me in the tree, explaining what I was doing there and how Callan scared off the wolves. Then I explained how we'd tumbled into the pack, causing it to fall into the river and how Callan had been carrying me most of the way. I didn't explain my ex, though. I wanted to wait for Callan to do that.

"I'm just grateful they're okay. That little girl means the world to all of us," Cohen replied, and I watched as he ran a hand over his face.

"Selina?" Callan called from over the hill.

"On my way!" I called back.

"Selina, pretty name," Cohen murmured.

"Oh, right. Sorry, I forgot to introduce myself," I apologized.

"Well, I saw you naked and forgot to ask, so we're even," he joked. I threw a wadded-up sock at him, and he laughed softly, bending to pick it up.

"Okay, I'm decent," I told him, painfully aware that I wasn't wearing a bra or panties, but there was nothing for it until I got back to camp and put my jacket on. Cohen turned back around and paused, his gaze running from my feet to my head. A cocky grin curved his lips, and he made a sound of approval.

"Whatever you're thinking, stop it," I warned, pointing a finger at him. His grin widened, but he said nothing as I collected my things. As intimidating as it was to be in a stranger's presence while naked, and as vulnerable as it could make a girl feel being on her own around such a man, I didn't feel the least bit worried around him. Cohen helped by scooping up my shoes and we started up the hill. I'd put fresh socks on when we got back.

"That was longer than ten minutes Seli—" the rest of Callan's words died when he spotted us.

"Cohen," he said with surprise and then he grinned.

"Uncle Cohen!" Mara squealed and ran from her shelter. I watched as Cohen knelt down and caught Mara on the fly, her little arms wrapping around his neck to hug him fiercely.

"Hey Angel-girl, did you miss me?" Cohen greeted, closing his eyes briefly in relief.

"Yes! We've been walking *so* much," she told him, pulling back.

"Thank Christ you found us," Callan called, stepping forward to greet his friend. Cohen shifted Mara to one arm and the guys gripped each other by the forearm and shook once, Callan's relief evident.

"You're telling me? The team is out here scouring the woods. When you didn't answer the SAT phone yesterday, we all got worried. West, Parker, Flinn, and Jason are all out here, we each picked a direction on the compass and started from the outside and have been hiking our way in. We figured we'd find you or at least a sign. I started seeing "*W's*" carved places and figured it had to be you. And when I caught sight of these little footprints," he said, tickling Mara who giggled adorably. "I was relieved to know you'd survived the storm."

"Well, as you can see, we have an addition to our—" Callan cut himself off, his eyes finally resting on me. I frowned and watched as his eyes traveled from my bare feet, bare legs and took in the long-sleeved men's shirt I was wearing.

"Why are you wearing Cohen's shirt?" he asked. I caught Cohen's amused look from beside me but ignored it. Instead, I crossed my arms over my stomach and glared.

"My clothes were wet, and he offered me a dry shirt," I answered.

"You were still bathing when he found you?" he clenched out.

"Jealous?" I poked.

Callan's glare lit a fire within me, and I struggled to keep the heat from my cheeks. To prevent this, I stepped past him to the camp where I could put on some warm socks.

"This is Selina," Mara introduced. I smiled at her as I carefully took a seat and slid on my socks without flashing anyone.

"She's gonna make sure Daddy's junk doesn't fall off."

I choked on air at her words and Callan dropped his head forward, running his hand through his thick hair. Cohen threw his head back and laughed, and my cheeks burned as Callan snuck a look at me that promised retribution. I have no idea how this was my fault, but that look sent a tingle through me anyway.

"Mara, what have we said about using that word?"

"To not to," she answered solemnly.

"Where did she learn that?" Cohen choked out.

"You and Jason, you fu—moron," Callan answered, refraining from swearing.

"Shoot, sorry man," Cohen said, but his grin said he thought it was hilarious.

Callan grabbed Mara and sat her in the shelter beside me and sighed.

"We were just about to sort food," Callan announced, ignoring his friend's pointed look.

"Oh, I brought MRE's," Cohen said, and pulled them out. For the next twenty minutes, we all sat in companionable silence and Callan filled Cohen in on most of the details and alluded to needing to talk about more when Mara was asleep. She had been kept in the dark for now about my ex, and we wanted it to stay that way.

"Well, now that you're here, I might quickly go and wash off and I'll be right back. You got any spare clothes?" Callan asked Cohen when we'd all finished.

"Selina has the shirt, but I have a set of pants," he answered and dug them out. I immediately felt guilty, but Callan waved me off, seeing the words on the tip of my tongue. Without another word, he scooped up the little bag with the soap and washer in it and jogged off into the fading light to wash off.

Cohen took a seat, and Mara regaled Cohen with tales of their camping trip. A few minutes later, my tongue glued itself to the roof of my mouth as Callan came striding back in clean pants and hiking boots, but with no shirt and just an unzipped jacket.

Holy mother of all things sinful.

Callan was ripped! Not that I didn't already have some idea of it—I'd been pressed up against him for the better part of two days—but I was *not* prepared for the sight of him with wet hair and no shirt, displaying rippling abs, solid pecs where one side was completely covered with a tattoo that I imagined had to link down to his arm. Did I mention he had only a light smattering of chest hair?

"You're gonna catch flies," Cohen murmured. I blinked quickly to clear my head and snapped my mouth shut, but not before I caught his knowing smirk. Callan's glittering eyes met mine and the corner of his mouth tilted up as if he knew exactly what I'd been thinking.

Without speaking, Callan hung his wet shirt beside mine on the branch I'd dragged over by the fire, and I had to force myself to look away.

"You look cold there, brother," Cohen pointed out with a shit-eating grin.

"I'll survive the night," he murmured before taking a seat a couple of feet away from me. My brain clicked into gear, and I moved for my pack.

"Oh, I forgot," I said and shuffled through it before handing him a shirt.

"You think your shirts will fit me?" he asked with a crooked smile.

"It's a shirt I used to sleep in, it's oversized and should fit you. I forgot it was in there," I explained.

Callan shook it out, and when he could see that it was big enough, he shrugged off his jacket and I was once again treated to all that toned, tanned skin. I was right, that tattoo did bleed down his left arm.

Callan pulled the shirt down and paused as he caught sight of the old, faded words. His gaze slowly rose to meet mine, understanding and empathy mixed in.

World's Best Dad! Was printed in faded and peeling words along the front.

"It was my dad's," I added unnecessarily.

"I can swap shirts if you'd prefer," he offered gently. I shook my head and smiled, but it felt a little sad.

"No, it's fine. I'm just glad it fits you," I answered.

"Your dad was a big man," Callan stated, pulling his jacket back on. I nodded and smiled again, this one real.

"He was. He grew up in the wilderness like this, him and his parents, and they ran a farm. He was almost six-foot-seven," I answered. Callan raised an eyebrow in surprise and looked me over again. I rolled my eyes and tossed a handful of leaves at him.

"My mother was five-foot-two," I answered his unasked question.

"Ah, so *she* was the short one. Not you at five-foot-three, that's right," he teased, and I laughed, remembering our argument yesterday. Sheesh, had we really only known each other for such a short time?

"So… you two really only met yesterday?" Cohen asked, raising an eyebrow. I turned back to him to see him looking between the two of us interestedly.

"Yes," Callan answered without any other explanation, so I just nodded.

"Huh… you just seem to know each other really well. History

and inside jokes…" He trailed off.

"Well, he did save my life and has been carrying me around for the last two days," I reminded. "

"And they were kissing," Mara piped up beside me tiredly. My face flooded with heat, and I refused to look at Callan, who I saw from the corner of my eye, dropped his head back to look at the starry night.

"Okay, munchkin, time for bed," Callan announced, standing up to scoop his daughter into his arms.

"But I'm not tired," she whined, which was predictably followed by a long yawn.

"Bed. Now," Callan ordered, sliding her in on the blanket.

"Can Selina sleep next to me?" she asked with another tired yawn. My eyes widened and flew to Callan who looked at me. I shrugged. If he was okay with it, then no way could I turn down that little girl's request.

"Mara…" He trailed off, running his hand over his damp hair. I could see his dilemma; he was worried Mara was getting too attached to me when he wasn't sure I'd be around much longer. I wanted to be upset at that, but he was just being a good dad, looking out for his daughter.

"Please, Daddy?" she begged. Callan seemed to be fighting with himself, and I stood up, brushing the leaves from my shirt.

"I don't mind," I whispered. Callan looked down at me, his eyes searching before he finally nodded and stepped back. I smiled and squeezed his arm in comfort before I carefully climbed in beside Mara, keeping her on the side closest to the fire.

"Yay!" she said, turning and snuggling into me. I hesitated a moment before I wrapped an arm around her and felt my heart melt all over again.

"I'm honored you wanted to cuddle with me," I told her, brushing her hair back gently.

"I like you," she murmured tiredly. Callan peered at us again before he stepped back and took a seat beside Cohen who was watching the whole interaction with knowing eyes and a smattering of sympathy.

"I like you too." I glanced back over at the guys and Callan started filling Cohen in about my situation.

"Can you keep playing with my hair?" Mara whispered sleepily.

"Of course, buttercup."

Her eyes fluttered closed, and she sighed gently. "That's what your daddy called you."

I smiled. "He did."

Another few moments passed, and she relaxed further.

"Can I be *your* buttercup?" she whispered. My chest tightened and I brushed a quick kiss over her head.

"Of course," I said softly as her breathing evened out.

"I wish you were my mommy," she mumbled before finally falling asleep.

Oh, baby girl. She was so hungry for female attention, for a mother. My heart broke for her because I knew all too well what that was like. I had been happy with my dad, and I never really felt like I went without, but I knew what it was to look at mothers and daughters, to see them on TV, to see my friends have it, to go through Mother's Day and have no one there to do any of it with.

"If I got to choose a little girl to be a mother to, I think I'd choose you," I murmured against her hair, knowing she was fast asleep and unable to hear me. Somehow, this little girl and her father had wormed their way inside my heart and had built themselves a space there. How? How, after such little time, had they done that?

It was sometime later when I raised my gaze to the guys and Callan tipped his head at me, silently asking if I was okay and I nodded my head.

I was fine right here.

Chapter Nine

CALLAN

"So, this fucker has just been stalking her for the last three years?" Cohen asked in a low voice.

I watched Selina in the shelter with Mara, the way she gently stroked her hair, her face full of emotion as she looked down at my daughter. I wanted so badly to know what they were talking about and what put that look of pain and love on Selina's face. I swallowed hard when she leaned forward and brushed a kiss over Mara's head.

"Yeah," I finally answered Cohen, turning my attention back to him. "He seems like a real nut-job, and I'm worried what he'll do if he gets his hands on Selina."

"Fuck," Cohen swore and scratched at his head.

"Hey, did you bring a SAT phone?" I asked.

"I already radioed in the guys. They set up for the night, but they'll leave before sun-up and meet us along the way," Cohen answered. My shoulders sagged in relief. Having my team out here with me made me feel more on my game, more capable of protecting my daughter and the unexpected woman with her.

My gaze traveled back to them, and Cohen sighed.

"She's beautiful, man, but she comes with a lot of baggage," he warned. I shrugged.

"Don't we all?"

"True. I just... I've never seen you this way with a woman before. I just wanted to make sure you're not caught up in being her hero and that your feelings are legit," he explained. I wanted to refute his statement, but I had to take it into consideration. I was a SEAL, and just because I wasn't operational didn't mean my instincts stopped being what I'd honed them to be. I protect; it was what I did. Was I just being seduced by the feeling of being the hero again?

"No," I shook my head. "No, it's nothing like that. *We're* nothing like that," I assured, even when a voice in the back of my head called me a liar.

"Sure you're not." He chuckled. "And what was it Mara said about you two kissing?"

I swore under my breath and threw a twig into the low fire.

"Exactly," Cohen continued. "Don't lie to yourself, man. There's something there. I haven't seen you tease a woman like that or take her feelings into such consideration in over six years."

"Doesn't mean anything. We both know this ends when we leave the forest," I muttered.

"Does it have to?"

I turned to look at him and frowned. "Are you trying to talk me out of starting something with her or not?"

Cohen shrugged. "It looks like you've already started something. I just want to make sure you're being real with yourself, whichever direction you go. The guys and I want to see you happy again, and fuck knows that little girl could probably benefit from having some estrogen around her in the next few years. But we'd hate for your first go out of the gate to crush you and stop you from trying again," he explained.

I considered his words carefully and had to admit he had a point. I had to be sure I was being honest with myself, whatever way I decided to go. It was pretty clear Selina and I had something, and for me at least, it was powerful and all-consuming. I hadn't felt anything like this for anyone so quickly before. I had to assume that our situation had something to do with the intensity, but there was a familiarity about her I couldn't shake.

Movement caught my attention, and I lifted my head to see Selina carefully climbing over Mara to get out of the shelter, the shirt riding up to show off miles of golden skin. I caught Cohen staring at her and I slapped him up the back of the head.

"Eyes to yourself, soldier," I growled low. Cohen laughed softly and dropped his gaze.

"She's hot."

"And not for you."

"Oh? Last I checked, when a woman wore your shirt with nothing under it, it was a pretty clear indicator who had dibs," Cohen quipped. I bit back another growl when Selina finally straightened, pulling the shirt back down around her knees and turning to look at us. She paused in the motion of shoving her hair away from her face, the action lifting her breasts beneath the shirt and dragging the material up her toned legs to mid-thigh.

Christ.

"Uh… I'm going to go for a quick walk," she told us after an awkward pause and heat stealing up her face.

"You shouldn't be walking around at night," Cohen pointed out. I rolled my eyes; the guy didn't understand subtleties.

"I'll go with you," I volunteered, climbing to my feet.

"No, it's fine. I can handle this on my own, thanks," she said, her bashfulness my undoing.

"I'm not going to stand right beside you, but I would like to be only a few feet away. Psycho ex, remember?"

She hesitated a moment and then nodded, avoiding my eyes as

she grabbed the little toiletry bag and hobbled away.

"Be back soon," I called to Cohen.

"Take your time. I got things here," he replied with a wink. If I could have thrown something at him, I would have.

I followed Selina a good distance away and turned to look at the camp. We were surrounded by trees and the fire was a good forty feet away, the stream ten feet to my left.

"You stay there," Selina told me. I leaned against the tree without question and watched as she ducked behind some bushes a few feet away.

"Talk to me," she called.

"About what?"

"Anything!" she cried, her voice full of embarrassment. I grinned and raked a hand over my hair.

"I don't like that Cohen saw you naked."

I heard her snort in laughter. "He didn't see me naked... at least, not really. I was fully submerged in the water."

"You mean the crystal-clear water?" I tossed out, looking at it as the moonlight shone on the dark surface.

"He didn't see anything," she assured. "Besides, what does it matter?"

"What do you mean, what does it matter?" I demanded, frowning.

"I mean," she said, coming out from behind the bush and heading for the water, still being careful of her injury. "Our kiss was a moment of weakness. I don't expect you're wanting more from me than that, so what does it matter if Cohen saw me naked?" she asked, washing her hands in the stream. I glowered at her, Cohen's words in my head clashing with my own desires. I was a fucking mess.

Selina gathered the little bag in her hand and started towards me. She gingerly stepped past me, and I snagged her hand and brought her around to face me. Her eyes were darker than normal in the bright moonlight, her skin luminous. Without pausing, I backed her up until her back hit the tree and her lips parted slightly.

"I don't like that you're wearing another man's shirt," I told her, my voice pitched low. Her body relaxed slightly, a smile teasing her lips.

"Are you jealous?" she asked, but her words were breathy.

"Fuck yes," I growled low, and I watched as her nipples pebbled beneath the thin material. I decided to explore this *thing* between us more. Her words were in my head, but they didn't sit right. I wanted more from her than that heated kiss. I wanted a whole hell of a lot more.

"Why?" Her breath hitched as I lowered my head to nuzzle her neck, breathing in the clean scent of her. I pressed against her, my cock hard and aching and she trembled slightly. I didn't fully comprehend *why* seeing her in Cohen's shirt pissed me the fuck off, only that it did. We didn't know each other, but we did. Somewhere over the last two days, I'd come to look at this woman as if I'd always known her... or maybe as if she was always meant to be here someday. Whatever was happening... it was potent, and I was ill-equipped to fight it.

"I don't like it," I whispered against her neck. Her skin broke out in little bumps, and she shivered against me. My hands teased the hem of the shirt where it rested an inch or so above her knees, and I groaned when she parted her legs enough for me to stand between them.

Her head tilted back slightly as I brushed a kiss on her neck, again and again, drowning in the scent of her, my body brushing against hers.

"Callan." My name came out part plea, part warning.

"Tell me to stop." My body was raging and my mind foggy. I

knew if she said to stop, I would, but right now, she was too tempting to resist, and the fact that she was wearing one of my best friends' shirts sent me into a wild mind-set where I needed to put my mark on her to warn off others. The fact that we barely knew each other, that I'd only known her for two days, or that she was trouble and likely to walk out of my life the moment we got out of these woods didn't matter. It only mattered that she, and any other man who saw her, knew she was mine... for however long that was.

"Tell me to stop, Selina, and I will," I promised, my fingers slowly dragging up her smooth thighs. Anticipation built, her breathing started coming faster and I could see her pulse jumping in her neck as I brushed my lips across the edge of her jaw.

"Tell me not to touch you, not to kiss you. Ask me not to taste you like I'm dying to," I continued, almost begging because one of us had to be the sane one here, and it apparently wasn't me. I rocked against her again, gently biting her neck.

"You have to be the one to tell me I have no right being jealous of you in another man's shirt. Tell me I shouldn't want to mark you in some way to make it clear that you're mine," I groaned, the feel of her hot, tight body against mine driving me wild.

"Please."

"Please what?" Did she want me to stop or keep going? My fingers traced higher, lifting the hem of her shirt. Her long lashes lifted as she looked up at me, her cheeks flushed and body radiating warmth.

"Don't stop."

Fuck!

I didn't give her another second to think. I leaned down to

kiss her, not wanting to give her a chance to back out or change her mind. I plundered, I took, our kiss ravaging and passionate. She made a small sound of pleasure in the back of her throat that made me want to howl with animalistic pride. *I* did that. I made her make that sound.

I slid my hands up further and paused, tearing my mouth from hers.

"Shit. Please tell me you haven't been sitting around the fire with Cohen not ten feet away... with no panties."

"They're drying," she answered. I swore again and kissed her hard, rocking myself against her in an effort to find some relief. Now wasn't the time for me, we didn't have the time... but I could touch her.

I slid my hands up her stomach to her breasts and she hissed, arching her back as I cupped them, my fingers stroking and teasing. Selina bit her lip, and I watched the desire build on her face. Wanting more, needing more, I tracked a hand back down and watched her eyes flutter again the lower I got.

She wasn't stopping me, and that knowledge had me hard enough to hammer nails. I leaned down to kiss her again, and at the same time slid my hand between her legs. She moaned and I swallowed the sound, stroking her, groaning at how wet she was, how slick and ready. Fuck, I wanted more. I wanted to slide inside her and make her scream my name until we were both spent. But I couldn't. Not now, not here. Her hips began to rock, and I kissed down her neck and then dropped to my knees.

"What are you doi—oh!" she gasped, slapping a hand over her mouth to muffle her moan as I buried my face between her legs. I gripped her injured leg and hooked it up over my shoulder and *feasted*. Fuck, she was amazing. Hot and wet, spiced honey on my tongue that I could eat forever. Her fingers slid to my hair where they bunched and tugged, her hips rocking and small gritted moans urging me on. I slid two fingers inside her and felt one of her hands leave my hair. When I looked up, she was covering her own mouth again, the sight was enough to leave my dick weeping.

Just her... this is just about her, I reminded myself. I was taking her scent on me, reminding her that she was mine, staking my claim in her mind and on her body.

Mine. Mine. Mine. With every thrust of my fingers and swipe of my tongue, I was claiming her. Her pleasure was my pleasure, and satisfaction seeped into me at watching her try to muffle her cries of ecstasy, something *I* was giving her.

"Callan." Her quiet moan turned my blood to molten lava, and I groaned against her, the action making her whimper. She was almost there; I could feel it. I slid another finger inside her and crooked my fingers, stroking her inside as I sucked on her clit.

"Callan!" Selina whisper-yelled before she shuddered, moaning low, her body arching and tightening. Watching her climb, watching her shatter and fall was *fucking spectacular.*
I didn't stop until every small shudder was wrung from her, and every ripple faded away. Taking one last lick at her, I brushed kisses up her thighs, her stomach, stopping for a moment to pay attention to those spectacular breasts before I dropped her shirt back down around her, tugging it until it covered her properly.

"Fuck, baby... watching you come is a thing of beauty," I praised and watched her eyes flutter open, and a lazy smile of satisfaction curved her lips. I felt a growl work its way up my throat and I kissed her again, unable to help myself. She kissed me back just as passionately, deeply.

"I want to put my scent on you like an animal. I want my cum all over you to mark you and keep other males away," I admitted harshly, and her brown eyes widened and heated, her lower lip between her teeth again.

"You could, you know," she panted. I swore under my breath and pressed my forehead to hers, clenching my teeth.

"You deserve more," I muttered against her lips. "We're not animals, and you're worth more than a quick fuck in a forest." Selina nipped at my lips and then pushed against my chest. I frowned and looked down at her, and she maneuvered us so that my back was against the tree. Her eyes were playful, her lips swollen, and cheeks flushed; she was gorgeous. Without warning, she grinned and then dropped to her knees in front of me, her hands on the button of my pants.

"Selina," I warned, tugging on her arm to bring her up again.

"You're not the only one who wants a taste," she replied breathily, and freed me from the confines of my pants.

"Wait. We shouldn't," I tried again, quickly losing any resistance to stop this. Her hand slipped inside and wrapped around my hard length, and I dropped my head back against the tree and gritted my teeth on the moan I wanted to let out. She stroked me slow and long, the feel of her hand on my cock almost enough to send me over the edge.

"Selina,." I said her name again as a last-ditch effort.

"Tell me to stop, Callan," she teased, her breath on my shaft.

"Tell me not to taste you, not to take you in my mouth and make you come," she urged, turning my words on me. I looked down at her, on her knees, the moonlight enough for me to see her flawless skin and deep brown eyes. Her dark hair was cascading over her shoulder and her smile was all sin.

"Don't stop," I rasped.

Eyes on me, she slowly pumped my length before lowering her mouth over me. Her tongue flicked out against the flared head of my shaft, and I bit back the moan that wanted to escape. With a pounding heart and anticipation rising, I watched as she slowly took me into her mouth, inch by inch of me disappearing into wet heat.

And then she sucked.

I clenched my fists at my side and sucked in a sharp breath, reminding myself not to be loud. Selina began to bob her head, taking me deeper into her mouth, her tongue swirling and her mouth sucking hard, her hand wrapped around the base of my shaft and stroking in time with her bobbing head. Fuck.

Time became irrelevant as she worked me like she knew all my weaknesses. My hips rocked forward gently in time with her sucking mouth, and I held off blowing, wanting to enjoy the moment even though I knew we didn't have a lot of time to waste. I watched her lips as they wrapped around my cock, sucking, stroking, her heavy lashes lifting so that her eyes clashed with mine. Goddamn... She was enjoying this. She wasn't just repaying the favor; this wasn't done out of obligation. The small moans in the back of her throat, the way she sucked and stroked as if it were her favorite thing to do...

"Selina... shit. Yes, just like that," I groaned low, sliding my hands into her silky hair. She moaned as I tugged gently and I took control, rocking my hips at the speed I needed, the depth I dared to go down her throat.

"Fuck, almost there," I warned, loosening my hold in case she wanted to pull away. She doubled her efforts, slipping a hand between my legs to stroke my balls.

"Fuck!" I almost snarled and hissed, and she sucked harder, faster, deeper. A tingle started at the base of my spine, my balls drew up and my breath became rapid. "Yes, yes, yes, fuck *yes!*" I bit out in pleasure, barely able to keep my voice down, shuddering, coming hard, stars bursting behind my eyes and my breathing strained. Selina sucked me deep, swallowing every drop of my cum, her moans of delight and encouragement making the experience that much hotter. Shit… she'd just taken my cum like she was hungry for it.

"That's my girl," I whispered somewhat reverently, stroking her hair, gently rocking my hips. Her hands continued to stroke, and she sucked on me hard one more time causing me to swear under my breath before she let my cock fall from her mouth.

I didn't wait for her to catch her breath, I pulled her to her feet and brought my lips crashing down on hers. She opened immediately and I barely refrained from devouring her. I wanted her again. Now. Hard and fast. I wanted to fuck her so deep she'd never get rid of me.

But…

I sighed and pulled away and she panted against me, a pleased smile curving her lips.

"Whatever you're thinking right now… hold onto that thought," she laughed quietly.

"I want more."

"Raincheck?" she asked. I pulled back slightly to look down at her flushed, upturned face and stroked a finger over her cheek.

"I'll hold you to that," I murmured before I kissed her again. This one was slower, softer, but I wanted to do it for hours until neither of us could breathe.

"We should get back," she reminded, pulling away. I nodded and she stroked my cheeks, her smile slightly bashful before she slipped by me to the water. I tucked myself back inside my pants and waited as she washed up, but instead of heading for the fire, she wandered back to me, her expression turning serious.

"What is it?"

It wasn't a look she should be wearing after just coming so hard she could have broken my fingers.

"I don't want to overstep... I just... I wanted to tell you something I noticed about Mara."

All lusty thoughts vanished, and I stiffened. "What about her? Is she okay?" I hadn't noticed any injuries when I bathed her before.

"Physically, she's fine," Selina hurried to assure. "It's just... something she said. And I can see it because I *was* Mara once upon a time."

"Okay," I trailed off, waiting.

"Please don't take this the wrong way, I just want to help," she continued. The longer she spoke without getting to the point, the more worry coiled in my gut.

"Mara is so special, and you have done such an amazing job with her. She is so well-adjusted and far smarter than any other six-year-old I know," she began. I waited. "I just... she's desperate for female attention, she's craving it so badly. It's not my place to tell you who to date or if you should or not... but I know you're worried about it and you're right. You need to be careful what woman you bring into her life. Because she is going to latch onto them like her life depends on it, and if they're not one hundred percent in that relationship with you... it's going to crush her if they leave."

I noted the shadow of sadness in her eyes, and I wondered if it was for my daughter, or at the idea of not being that woman. My heart sank at her words. It was something I was already aware of, already cautious of, but hearing from a woman who'd grown up with a single dad and a dead mother just confirmed it all for me.

"I know," I finally admitted, my voice rough.

Selina smiled gently at me before she nodded once and started towards the camp. I ran a hand over my hair and exhaled slowly. She was right... and that's why we couldn't happen. Selina was young, free-spirited, and had a lot of her own troubles and baggage. No matter how much I wanted her... my daughter came first, both in her emotional needs and in matters of her safety. And with Selina's life the way it was right now... I couldn't take the risk. Mara was already getting attached to her...

I would have to let her go.

With that bitter thought, I slowly followed behind her, ready to get this night over with.

Chapter Ten

CALLAN

I was first up the next morning. I hadn't slept well anyway, worries over the psycho stalker and Mara's well-being kept me awake. Not to mention the feeling of loss where Selina was concerned. I didn't know her, but I did. And knowing I had to let her go left me feeling like I'd lost something amazing before I'd even really had a chance to explore it.

We had serious chemistry, that was as obvious as the forest around us. She was intelligent and eager to learn, independent and strong-willed. There was definitely potential for us to be more.

But Selina was right, I had to be careful... for Mara's sake.

I had a quick breakfast ready for everyone by the time they all got up, most of our supplies were already packed away. I wasn't hungry and skipped breakfast, and instead planned the places we'd stop today before getting home. Knowing we were so close was a relief... and a disappointment. Because once we got home, I'd have to say goodbye to Selina. We would call the local authorities and get them to do their jobs and look after her. Lucas was the Deputy Sheriff and a friend of mine, so I knew he'd look out for her. But I would have to let her go after that, and we wouldn't see her again. Because she was right; I needed to be certain of the woman I brought into Mara's life, and I was never going to be certain. I wasn't sure what it would take to give me that level of assurance, but I didn't think it would ever happen.

"You look like shit," Cohen pointed out as I rolled the tent and sleeping bag up, stowing them away in the pack. I grunted my response, my gaze trailing to Selina where she was helping Mara to make another flower crown. They were both grinning and an ache formed in my chest when Mara giggled, and Selina smiled warmly at her.

"Anything you care to share?"

"No."

"So you don't want to talk about whatever it was you and the lovely Selina got up to last night when you were gone for so long?"

"No."

"You're going to let her go, aren't you?" Cohen pushed.

"This falls under the shit that isn't any of your business," I snarled, tightening the straps to the pack.

"All I'm saying, Cal, is to not throw away a good thing out of fear," he added softly. I didn't bother responding. We had about forty minutes before the sun started to rise, and I wanted to be well on our way by then.

"Alright guys, last chance for a bathroom break because we need to get going," I called out. Selina nodded and placed the newly finished crown on Mara's head before getting carefully to her feet. My gut clenched as her dark eyes met mine and she smiled softly.

Moments of last night flashed in my head, our first kiss, the way she tasted on my tongue, the feel of her pussy clamping hard on my fingers, the sound of her coming, and the little noises of pleasure she made... fuck. I could still feel the way she took my cock like she was made for it, the way she played my body like she owned me.

There was the sound of her laughter, the warmth in her voice when she spoke to me, and the adoration in her expression when she looked at my daughter. I loved the way she arced up and got mouthy when she was all indignant… the way she felt when I carried her…

Too soon. All of this had happened too soon. I couldn't trust it.

"Cohen, can you carry Mara, please? I'd like to cover some ground today," I asked, shaking my head to get rid of those thoughts.

"Sure, but are you sure you don't want me to carry Selina and give you a break?" he offered. I could hear the sincerity in his voice, but I hated the idea of another man carrying her.

"It's fine," I replied shortly. Cohen raised an eyebrow but didn't comment further.

Without giving her much more warning, I swept Selina up in my arms and tried to squash how right it felt to have her there.

"You okay?" she whispered. I glanced down at her big brown eyes and almost drowned there.

"Yeah, just ready to be home," I answered shortly and glanced away. I caught her small frown from the corner of my eye, but I couldn't let it affect me. I knew she wasn't mine to keep, and I knew I was confusing her by running hot and then cold, but damn it… I had to start putting some emotional space between us or it was going to be a shit-show when we said goodbye.

Fuck, it was already going to be hell letting her go.

~

SELINA

Callan was pulling away from me.

I wasn't sure if it was just that his friend was now with us, or if he took my words to heart last night. But whatever was going on, he was pulling away, shutting me out and making me feel like the burden I already was with him carrying me. I'd asked to walk myself several times only to be met with a glower. Cohen had offered to carry me, but Cal had ignored him.

I frowned at his shirt as we walked… my shirt. My dad's shirt.

Okay, it was really soon to be this worked up about the guy, but… we had something, didn't we? I inwardly winced and wanted to dunk my own head into a pond of water. I sounded so pathetic, so predictable.

We had a connection. Gag! I wanted to slap myself.

We had known each other for almost three days, and it had been pretty intense. He had saved me. He represented safety. Watching him with Mara had reminded me of my own dad and caused me to contrive this version of him in my head so that I felt more for him than I should. He was my savior, and I was feeling gratitude more than anything… that had to be it. Only…

I sighed. I could still feel the way he touched me, intimate, hot, expertly. A tingle started down low and I gritted my teeth. I could taste him in my mouth, feel how well he filled me, feel the heat and texture of his body. I almost groaned at the memory of his hands in my hair as he took control and used me to get off. Making him come had gotten me so hot and wet again, I'd wanted to climb him like a tree and let him have his way with me. But out here wasn't the time or the place. And now… I was sure we'd missed our chance.

Then there was the way he looked at me, like I was *worth*

protecting and being here for. And Mara? My heart clenched as I glanced at the chattering little girl in Cohen's arms. How could I not love her already? She was everything innocent and pure, and so damned cute.

But Callan was preparing to say goodbye. I knew it, and I hated it. *I* was the moron who let herself get too attached to a practical stranger. This pain I was feeling, the pain I was *going* to feel, was all on me. I had no one to blame but myself. I sighed again and Callan tightened his arms around me.

"You okay?"

"Fine," I answered without looking at him.

"I may not have had a relationship with a woman for six years, but as I recall, when a woman says she's *fine* she's anything but."

I refused to let out the smile that threatened. He wasn't allowed to be all cute and charming when he was pushing me away and distancing himself. No.

"I really am fine, Callan. I'm just tired and ready for this whole thing to be over."

And I was tired—of all of it—even him. Maybe even especially him. Because this slow torture of waiting for him to say goodbye, to push me away, was worse than him simply rejecting me and saying this isn't going to happen. I could see he wanted me; I could see he was tempted. But me and my big mouth had to remind him to be careful where Mara was concerned, and now he was fighting with himself, reminding himself it was best for Mara and that I had too much baggage, too much evil attached to me to bring me into his daughter's life.

And he was right.

"Are you sure?" Callan asked again.

"Yep. Hey, are we going to stop soon? Your back must be

killing you," I asked, desperate to change the subject.

"Cohen?" Callan called. "Where are the guys?"

"Not far. We can stop soon, and they'll find us," Cohen called back.

"Five minutes," Callan replied. Cohen signaled that he'd heard, and I watched as Mara adjusted her little flower crown before continuing her saga on what she thought school would be like.

"Selina…" Callan trailed off with a heavy tone.

"Don't," I cut him off quickly, ducking my head. I watched his throat bob as he swallowed, and I shook my head.

"Just… don't. Please?"

His arms tightened around me for a moment, and I watched him from beneath my lashes, watching the struggle on his face as he tried to think of what to say. But we both knew how this was going to go and why, no words needed to be said.

We stopped in a small clearing a few minutes later and Mara came skipping over to me. We'd made a lot of progress and the sun was just coming up, and the air had that fresh, crisp smell to it. I took a small drink of water as I watched Cohen and Callan talk quietly amongst themselves. My attention shifted to the area around us, and I wondered if I'd see any sign of Patterson. I never had before, and it was worrying that we were out here with almost no protection. Patterson was scary, and he wanted me back. I was his favorite toy, the thing he loved to make scream for his own pleasure. I never wanted to go back.

Never.

There was a rustling ahead and we all fell silent. I watched as Callan and Cohen stiffened and turned in the direction of the noise. I stood shakily and grabbed my rifle, stepping in front of Mara. More rustling and low voices.

Callan turned back to look for Mara and I stepped aside slightly so he could see her behind me. He sent me a grateful smile before looking back in time to see three large men step out of the trees.

"Uncle Flynn, Uncle West, Uncle Jason!" Mara squealed before scrambling to her feet and running at them. I watched grins break out on the faces of the men and the first one caught her in a tight hug before handing her wiggling body over to the next. Each of them hugged her fiercely before stepping forward to shake hands with Cohen and Callan.

"Fuck, it's good to see you, man. You had us worried," one of them greeted.

"Yeah, I lost my pack with everything in it, including my SAT phone," Callan replied, and I noted the warmth in his voice, the change in him.

"How the hell did that happen?" the man asked.

"Uh," I interrupted, and several pairs of eyes swung to look at me. "That would be my fault."

"And who are *you, Piccola?*" The one who'd spoken asked, his dark brown eyes running over me appreciatively, the scruff on his face enhancing his masculine features, a crooked smile that would charm all the ladies flashed. His Italian accent was heavily put on, but I had no doubt he spoke the language fluently.

"Jason," Cohen snapped a warning.

"I'm Selina... otherwise known as the woman who fell out of a tree and onto your friend. He was helping me to the stream when I stumbled into his bag and knocked it into the water," I answered as Jason stepped closer.

"Why were you in a tree?" he asked.

"Why is that everyone's first question?" I asked with a pout. Jason chuckled and I swallowed hard. Oh lordy, I felt that soft laugh in places down low.

"I'm a nature photographer. I'd been in the tree for hours waiting to get a particular photo, and I was preparing to leave my tree when a random mountain man arrived, so I paused, not wanting to draw attention to myself because I didn't want to be left alone with a strange man in the woods. I was going to wait until he left when my arms gave way and I fell. Right on top of him," I explained with a smile.

"Ah, you fell for the wrong SEAL, *mi amore*," he flirted, waggling his eyebrows.

"Can we get moving?" Callan interrupted us sharply. I glanced at him with a small frown, but his face was impassive. Cohen rolled his eyes behind his friend and the others appeared perplexed.

"Sure. Do you need a lift, *il tesoro?*" Jason asked, holding out his impressive arms. Jesus… were all these men so perfect?

"Lay off the Italian, Jason." Cohen sighed with a grin.

"Uh…" I trailed off, looking at Callan, half hoping he'd demand to hold me again.

"Jason can carry you for a while, we need to get going," he mumbled darkly before stepping past his friends. They all looked between me, and Callan and I ducked my head.

"Stubborn jackass," Cohen mumbled. I glanced up at him and he flashed me a quick, dimpled smile. "Don't take it personally, sweetheart. He can be dense sometimes," Cohen added before following his friend.

"I'm Flynn," one of the guys stepped forward to introduce himself. He had eyes as green as moss and black hair that only made them stand out more. I smiled and shook his hand, noting the light scar that ran from his temple to his jawbone.

"I'm the handsome one, they call me West," another one greeted, dark blonde hair longer than the other guys' with pale blue eyes and features better suited to a runway model than a soldier with the exception of his nose that was slightly crooked, as if it had been broken and not healed properly.

A girl could get dizzy amongst these fine men.

"Nice to meet you all. Isn't there one of you missing?" I asked, wondering where the other teammate was I'd heard Cohen mention last night.

"Parker stayed back with Mara's grandparents to help coordinate the search," Jason explained.

"What's up Callan's ass, anyway?" Flynn asked. I shrugged and shifted my gaze guiltily.

"It's been a long few days, and we haven't had it easy. I'm afraid I compounded that with my stalker-ex situation," I explained feeling guilty.

"Oh yeah, Cohen explained that over the SAT phone. He's following you?"

"I'm not sure if he's following us now, but he was. And Callan swore he felt someone following us yesterday and the day before," I answered. The guys looked at each other with unease and then Jason smiled.

"Oh well, let's get out of here, and then we can deal with that situation. I'll give you a lift," he offered.

"I got second," Flynn said quickly.

"Fine, save the best and most impressive for last," West said with a wink, and I laughed. They were a good-looking, flirty bunch, but I got the impression they meant nothing by it.

Jason carefully picked me up, and I felt a little awkward in his arms compared to Callan. With Callan, I could sink into him, hold him close and it felt natural. But with Jason, it didn't feel like I could be as personal with him.

"Alright, *Piccola*, let's get you back home," Jason said softly.

West and Flynn walked on either side of us but slightly ahead, and I got the impression that I was being guarded. I could see Callan and Cohen a little further up, Mara in Callan's arms. A small twinge of wistfulness hit me, and I dragged my gaze to Jason's chest. I hated that he was pushing me away, but I understood.

"So… I'm not imagining the tension here between you and our old CO, am I?" Jason asked. I tipped my head back to look at his handsome face and inwardly sighed. He was gorgeous, his Italian heritage shining through that roguish smile.

"I don't know what you're picking up between us," I answered.

Jason scoffed. "I take that to mean things got very intense. It doesn't take a genius to see that he's smitten with you."

"We barely know each other," I mumbled without looking at him.

"And yet there is the undercurrent of something more. From what Cohen told us… you two have gotten pretty close these last few days. I know intense situations can make these feelings bigger, but that doesn't mean they aren't real," he explained with a shrug.

"Look… Callan doesn't want to talk about it, so I won't either," I answered kindly.

"Cohen said that Mara mentioned you two kissed," Jason continued as if I hadn't spoken.

"While we're on the subject of things that Mara has said, you need to watch your mouth around her," I scolded, poking him in the chest. His wide eyes turned to me, and he frowned.

"Why?"

"I believe she overheard you telling Callan that if he didn't get laid soon, that his junk would fall off," I bit out. Jason laughed and shrugged.

"So?"

"So… Callan and I had known each other for a whole of ten minutes before she asked if I was going to make sure his junk didn't fall off," I explained.

Jason stumbled slightly, and the other guys snickered. Jason laughed and shook his head.

"Shit, she said that?"

"Yes. And then she told Cohen that I was going to have that honor too."

"Well… are you?" Flynn asked with a grin. I stiffened and shook my head.

"You're all as bad as each other," I muttered under my breath. He grinned and West laughed.

"We're just looking out for our buddy. The guy doesn't date, and he has made it clear that Mara is the only girl in his life. But he can't keep on like that, and we want to see him happy. The fact that he totally ignored you before, those little looks and undercurrents… that tells us he's feeling things *big time,*" West continued.

"Yeah, well." I shrugged. "My life isn't something he needs to get suckered into right now. Besides, he doesn't want to feel things, and I'm pretty sure we're over before we even begin," I grumbled, trying not to feel so hurt at that. It had only been a few *days*. I needed to stop sulking over this, because really, everything that had happened made it hard to decipher if what we were feeling was just in the moment or if it had any chance of surviving the monotony of real life.

"Give it time," Flynn suggested with a small wink. "It always did take the big guy a little longer to clue into his own feelings."

I chuckled lightly at his use of the words *big guy*. They were *all* big.

"How do you get on with Mara?" West asked. I smiled and

shrugged, my chest warming at the thought of that little girl. My gaze traveled back to her as she turned to look at us. Her smile grew wide, and she waved enthusiastically, causing Callan to turn around and look at us. My smile dimmed slightly as his eyes locked with mine.

Jason whistled low and sighed. "Yeah, Cal is feeling it. He's just fighting it, but he'll come around. And it looks like Mara likes you enough."

I wish you were my mommy.

Her sleepily whispered words came back to me, but I kept them to myself. I wouldn't give these guys any ammunition to influence Callan in any way. If he wanted to see where things went when we got back to reality, then I was all for it. But I didn't want him to do it because his daughter wanted us together.

"We'll stop in about an hour for a small break. We should be back at the house well before sunset," Cohen called back to us. The guys indicated that they'd heard and continued on walking. My gaze slid back to Callan, his back still to me, his posture stiff, and I tried to guard my heart against the blow I knew was coming.

Chapter Eleven

CALLAN

"Nana! Pop!"

Mara flew from my arms and up the stairs of our back porch into the waiting arms of her grandparents. They both dropped to their knees and wrapped her up tight, their relief at seeing her safe and sound was obvious.

"Good to see you still alive," Parker greeted with a grin, stepping down to shake my hand. I noticed that his limp was a little more pronounced today, which meant he'd been on it a little too long, pushing himself.

"Good to see you too, man," I replied, meaning it as I clapped him on the back.

"You had us worried there, son," Lyle, my father-in-law, told me, stepping forward. I was glad I'd never had a falling out with Lina's parents. Lyle only called me *son* when he was worried or serious.

"I was a little worried too, to be honest, but I knew we'd get home okay. It was a relief to know my team would come looking if they couldn't get a hold of us," I admitted, shaking the older man's hands.

"And I see you didn't come back empty handed," he added, smiling kindly over my shoulder.

"Hi," Selina greeted with a soft smile, uncertainty printed all over her face.

"Hey, darlin'. I heard you've had quite the experience. I'm Lyle, Mara's grandfather," my father-in-law greeted, holding out his hand as West gently put her on her feet. We'd only stopped three times today, and each of the guys had taken a turn carrying Selina to help us move faster. I had loathed every moment of it, knowing their hands were on her, but I knew it was for the best. I had refrained from carrying her again since this morning. I could see that my distance was hurting her, but we both knew this was for the best.

"I did. I'm grateful Callan was out there and that his friends were so nearby," Selina answered.

"How bad is your ankle? My wife used to be a nurse up until seven years ago and can take a look at it for you," Lyle offered.

"Not so bad. It's on the mend. But we didn't want to risk me walking and setting it back again."

"Well, let's get you all inside. I think Mara could do with a good bath, and Eileen has been cooking all day in preparation for you getting back in time for dinner," Lyle added, waving everyone towards the house. The guys all moved forward at the promise of food, leaving me the only one there to help Selina.

She smiled awkwardly, and I could see the guard in her eyes go up.

"Want a hand?" I offered. She shook her head.

"No, I can manage," she refused and began limping towards the patio. I sighed in exhaustion and exasperation at her stubborn refusal to accept my help, and quickly swept her up in my arms and strode after the group. They were all inside already.

"You can put me down," she murmured low as I hit the steps.

"May as well carry you inside," I replied, trying to soak in the feeling of her in my arms again while I could.

"Seriously, Cal. Put me down, I'm fine," she ordered, and I could *hear* the way she was holding herself back. Gritting my teeth, I did as she requested and slowly let her down, her body sliding down the front of mine. Her gaze flew to my face, her eyes wide and lips parted, and it took all my strength not to lean down and kiss her again.

"You should back up," she whispered.

"Yeah…" I trailed off, distracted by the feel of her smooth skin on my fingertips where they rested on her hips. Her shirt had ridden up slightly and I wanted to pull her towards me, hold her closer.

"Cal, please," she pleaded softly, and it wasn't until I looked at her face again and saw the way she was struggling to keep emotion off her face that reality came slamming back into me.

"I'm sorry," I told her gently, and we both knew I wasn't apologizing for holding her too long. Her expressive face reflected her hurt and she shrugged a shoulder and attempted a smile.

"I know. Me too." Her voice was rough and her expression sorrowful. I slid my thumb over the smooth skin of her cheek, and she leaned into my touch a little.

"It's only been a couple of days… are we crazy for feeling like this?" I asked. I was glad that she didn't play games and or ask me to specify my feelings. I could recognize how strongly she felt about me, and I could see she knew my feelings too.

"Usually I would say yes. But… I don't feel like I've known you for only three days, Cal. Maybe we stepped into some kind of time loop or something, but I *know* you," she answered, shrugging softly, trying to smile as if the truth was more interesting than painful.

"If things were different…"

"Maybe, but they're not, and so we can't," she finished for me, her dark eyes filled with sadness and weariness.

"And Mara—"

"Is a lucky girl to have a father like you. You're doing great, Cal, and I love that she's your priority... as she should be," she assured. Her words should have made me feel better, they should have filled me with reassurance that I was doing the right thing and that I wasn't ruining a rare chance with an incredible woman.

But they didn't.

Feeling eyes on us, I flicked my attention inside to see everyone in the kitchen staring at us with avid interest.

"Shit," I murmured with a sigh and shook my head. Selina glanced over too, and they all jumped into action, trying to hide that they'd been watching us. She laughed low and shook her head before turning to me again.

"I should be getting home. Can one of your guys give me a lift?" she asked. I frowned and shook my head.

"No. You need to wait for the Deputy to get here. We can't just let you go off on your own when your psycho ex is hanging around," I reminded.

Any laughter in her eyes vanished and she stiffened and pulled away slightly.

"He's why I need to put some distance between us," she explained.

"Selina... we can't just drop you off and say goodbye. What if he hurts you? I wouldn't be able to live with myself if that happened and I could have done something to stop it. Just wait here for the Deputy. You can tell him everything and we'll make sure you're given protection," I explained, determined to abduct her to keep her safe if that was what it took.

I watched indecision war on her face, shadows and memories washing over her until she breathed out heavily and nodded.

"Fine. But I'm leaving tonight, one way or the other," she

relented, her jaw set and eyes intense.

"You're cute when you're serious," I murmured, feeling one side of my mouth curl in a smile. Her gaze dropped to my mouth, and she shook her head.

"Stop being charming. I'm trying not to like you," she muttered. I grinned and she shook her head. "And while you're at it, stop smiling too. It's hard enough without seeing that smile," she glared. I attempted to wipe the smile from my face, but I knew I was unsuccessful when she sighed in exasperation and shook her head, her eyes laughing.

"Come on, let's go eat. Eileen cooks amazing roasts and I'm starving," I suggested. Nodding, Selina let me lead her into the house and to a seat where Eileen placed a plate in front of her and showered her with attention and questions.

Mara quickly joined Selina at the table and regaled her grandmother with stories on how Selina fell out of the tree and how she made flower crowns. Watching Mara with her... it should have felt wrong, worrying, disorienting.

But everything just felt... right.

~

SELINA

Mara's grandparents were amazing. They were so warm and welcoming, so open to questions without being invasive in return. Eileen checked out my ankle and re-wrapped it, but she agreed that it was on the mend and that I just needed to rest up. The guys were hilarious, and kept up a steady stream of commentary that had us all laughing and the tension in the room fading. Eileen's roast was amazing, and I wasn't just saying that because I'd had packet food the last week and a half or because I hadn't had a home cooked meal made by someone else since before my dad died. She explained that she had started taking some culinary courses and wanted to open up her own little restaurant in the next three years. Judging by that one meal I'd had, I figured she had a good chance at making it work.

Mara had been bathed, her hair braided, and she was curled up next to me on the enormously comfortable couch while I stroked her head. I needed to get going, I had to leave. Callan had called the Deputy an hour ago, but he said he'd be a little while yet as he had another situation he was dealing with.

"Are you going to go home now?" Mara asked softly. I glanced around; Eileen and Lyle were in the kitchen cleaning, Callan and the guys on the porch situated behind me, talking over some drinks. I knew they were distracted though, since I could hear them all easily. I cleared my throat and took a deep breath.

"Yeah, buttercup. I need to get back to my own home now," I answered softly.

"You won't stay with us?" she asked, playing with the little stuffed animal in her hands.

"I don't live here," I reminded.

"But you could."

I forced a smile and shook my head. "I have my own house, honey, with my own stuff. You and your dad have a life out here," I tried to explain. She was silent for a moment, and I waited while she thought, because if there was one thing I'd learned about Mara, it was that she didn't just drop a subject.

"I don't want my dad to be alone," she admitted softly. My hand stopped stroking for a moment as her words sunk in. They were the words I used to think as a kid, watching my dad do everything alone and never find love.

"Hey," I whispered, tugging her up so that she turned to look at me. "Listen... Your daddy is a very strong and capable man. He loves you with *all* his heart, and as long as you are happy and healthy and thriving, then he will never be unhappy," I assured her.

She shrugged. "But I'm going to school soon, and daddy will be alone a lot."

"Do you see all the uncles you have out there? And your Nana and your Pop? They all love your daddy and will make sure he's not lonely. You don't need to worry about that, it's a grown-up responsibility," I tried to assure.

"Did you ever have another mommy?" she asked softly, her big blue eyes so sad it was heartbreaking.

I put a smile on my face and shook my head.

"Nope. It was just me and my dad, and I loved it. He was happy with just me, and we had a lot of fun together. I got to learn things no other girl my age knew," I explained, trying to make it sound like it was all that mattered.

Her intelligent eyes studied me, and I waited.

"Did you ask my daddy if you could be my mommy?" she asked softly. I stiffened and shook my head, worried she'd be upset with me.

"Why?" she asked with a small frown. "Don't you want to be a mommy?"

"Mara..." I began and brushed a red lock from her face. "You are the most amazing little girl in the whole wide world. You really are, and that makes you *so* special. And a girl as special as you needs a mommy who is just as special and amazing. Your dad is already there, and so he needs to be super sure that if you get another mommy... that she deserves you," I explained, feeling out of my depth and scrambling.

"I think you would be an awesome mommy," she defended. I smiled and shook my head.

"I'm flattered you think so. Coming from you, that's an amazing compliment." I grinned.

"So… will you ask?" she questioned, her big eyes hopeful.

"How about we just leave it up to your daddy to pick your mommy, okay? He knows what's best," I diverted with a small laugh.

"But I want *you* as my mommy," she pouted, crossing her arms over her chest. I opened my mouth to respond when there was a sharp inhale behind me. Mara's eyes widened and her arms dropped, and I didn't need to turn around to know who was there.

I swung my legs over the couch quickly and turned to see Callan standing there, Jason at his back, both of them staring at us with wide eyes. Jason's expression was something along the lines of *oh shit*, where Callan's was a mix of emotions.

"Cal—"

Then the lights went out, plunging us into darkness.

Mara's arms wrapped around me tightly, and I held her close, waiting for my eyes to adjust in the moonlit room. There was movement around us, and I watched as several dark forms came closer. I wasn't worried though, I knew they were Cal's teams.

"Everyone to the lounge, now," Callan's deep voice commanded. More movement, and as everyone crowded forward, I could make out their expressions.

"You think it's him?" West asked.

"Has to be," Jason answered.

"You got equipment?" That was Parker this time.

"As if he doesn't have equipment," Cohen scoffed.

"This way. Selina, bring Mara, we're putting her in the safe room," Callan answered tensely.

"Okay," I agreed breathily, and climbed to my feet with Mara clutched in my arms, her little legs wrapped around me. My ankle was throbbing and ached immediately, but I couldn't think about that right now. Adrenaline had kicked in, and I was worried what would happen next. I was hemmed in by six large men as we walked down the dark hallway. I was a little surprised that Callan had a safe room, but really, I shouldn't have been. The man was serious about protecting his daughter. Knowing that all this was only happening here because of me made me feel insanely guilty.

Because there was no way what was happening now didn't have anything to do with me and Patterson.

We reached the end of the hall where a single door stood, and Callan hurriedly punched in the keys and opened it. The room was small, smaller than our cave, and there were supplies everywhere. Callan grabbed a heavy looking bag off the top shelf and passed it to Cohen, who slid it to the ground and unzipped it before he began passing out guns to his teammates. I gaped at the hardware in there and shook my head. He was a SEAL, weren't they always prepared for the worst-case scenario?

"Lyle, Eileen, I want you guys in here with Mara and Selina," Callan told them, helping the older couple over the threshold.

"I shouldn't be in there," I said quickly.

"I don't have time to argue this, Selina," Callan gritted out. I sighed and looked down at Mara and kissed her forehead.

"I'll see you soon, buttercup, okay? Stay here with your Nana and Pop."

Her arms clung tighter, and she frowned. "I want you too."

I nodded. "I know, baby girl, but I need to help your daddy with this. So, you wait in here, and I'll be back soon."

"Promise?" she asked, her blue eyes wide and frightened. I swallowed hard and forced a smile.

"Promise," I whispered, even though I knew it was one I would likely have to break.

Mara leaned up to kiss my cheek gently before she let me pass her to her grandparents. Eileen's wide eyes were searching my face and I gave her what I hoped was a reassuring smile.

"Selina," Callan warned.

"Shut the door so we can talk," I told him quickly. Clenching his jaw, Callan quickly kissed Mara and ran through the instructions and codes with his in-laws before closing the door.

"Patterson is after *me*, I shouldn't be anywhere near them."

"He can't get into the safe room. You being in there means we know where he'll try to break into, and we'll have a better chance of catching him," Callan refuted.

"What you have a better chance of is him maybe taking out a few of your guys and then disappearing to come back and fight another day. You can't be with me forever, and he knows that. He can and will wait us out. If there's one thing Patterson has in abundance, it's patience. We can use me as bait right now and catch him," I explained.

Callan opened his mouth to reply but Cohen cut in.

"She has a point, Callan. The guy is ballsy if he's going to try and play with us when he can see how many of us are here. The Sheriff's department isn't equipped to handle this."

"Selina—"

An explosion sounded nearby, and I ducked out of instinct. Callan was there, hovering over me, pushing me down to cover me. I peered around nervously and heard gunfire.

"Over here!" came Jason's shout before gunshots sounded.

Chapter Twelve

SELINA

"Stay in the house, here behind the couch. Stay hidden," Callan ordered me as Cohen, Flynn, and West went running past to help their teammate.

"But—" I tried, and he cut me off with a quick, hard kiss.

"Stay out of sight so we know you're safe. I don't want to risk you accidentally getting shot because you were in the wrong place. If you're in here, I know where you are." His blue eyes burning with intensity. He was calm, collected, not panicked and shaky. He was a leader ready to lead. His voice was authoritative and commanding, and I felt myself already bending to it.

"Selina." He said my name quickly, a small demand for an answer.

"I'll stay here," I promised. He searched my face quickly before he nodded, cupped my face briefly and then left. I watched him move on silent feet, his solid bulk not making a sound, his movements fluid.

The gunfire was coming from the back of the house, and I wondered how they were going to take Patterson out.

"Does he work alone?" Parker asked, sliding up beside me. I had noticed Parker walked with a pronounced limp, and I had to assume he had an injury that prevented him from hiking out to help find us the other day.

"Always," I answered quickly, my heart hammering. "He's

never gotten along with anyone, which is why his job as a hacker suits him so well."

"Great. Antisocial and sadistic," Parker muttered, loading a magazine into his gun. He flashed me a quick, reassuring smile, patted my arm and crawled past me on his belly to help his friends. I licked my lips and looked around, wondering what I could do to help. I didn't want to go back to Patterson, I would rather die. But he was here now because of me. Callan and his friends were risking their lives because of me, and it had to stop. I had to get out of here, draw Patterson away before any of them got hurt or died. He may be just one man, but he was far more intelligent than they were giving him credit for. It felt like my heart was working its way out of my chest at the idea of being with that man again, but what other choice did I have?

"There's two shooters!" I heard one of the guys call out. I frowned and stood carefully, trying to see the battle outside. "Coming from the west and north!" someone else shouted. "Round 'em up, split into two. Bravo two and three are with me, the rest of you head to the west," Callan ordered. I didn't need to see the others to know they followed his orders without question. They may all be retired from the Navy, but Callan was still their leader.

I frowned at the thought of two shooters. Patterson *never* worked with anyone else, he didn't play well with others. Even when we'd been together, he'd wanted me to follow his lead in all things, and when I didn't, he became cruel. It didn't make sense for him to have a partner now. That was another thing... Why wait until there were so many of us here to attack? Why hadn't he started picking us off in the forest when it would have been harder to defend ourselves? Although, that part kind of made sense now that I thought about it. Patterson always did like a challenge and never bothered to help companies whose security was so easy that it took less than ten minutes to break into. No, he loved to know he broke through protections that were supposed to guard secrets and important details. It was an ego boost and something he thrived on, fed off.

The constant gunfire kept my breathing working rapidly and my heart pounding out at an unsteady pace. I could still hear the guys calling out orders and comments, but their words were harder to understand as they moved further from the house.

Further from the house...

My back stiffened, and my breath caught when I realized what he'd done... what he was doing. Patterson worked alone, he loved a challenge... and he was a hacker. Being here on Callan's home-turf was the ultimate *fuck you* to the military, a group who had kicked him out for being unstable. Taking them down while outsmarting them on their land was going to give him the ultimate satisfaction.

Scrambling to my feet, my ankle screaming, I ran onto the back patio.

"He's not out there! It's a trap!" I shouted, hoping they heard me over the gunfire before I whirled around and ran for the kitchen.

It was only the thought of protecting Mara and Callan that forced my knees to keep me upright when fear had them threatening to collapse. I opened a drawer and drew out a sharp knife used to cut up fruit. It was small, small enough that I could palm it and not be obvious.

The sounds of gunfire remained steady, but I could no longer hear Callan or his men. They were okay, they had to be. *Please be on your way back...*

"Come on, Selina. Move it," I whispered to myself.
Straightening my spine, I walked quickly across the kitchen,
through the living room and down the hall that led to the safe
room. As soon as I saw the light spilling out on the floor from
the open door, dread flooded through me, but I also felt
something settle. There was no choice now, and the path I had
to take was clear.

As I got closer, I could see Eileen and Lyle on the ground just
inside the safe room. Lyle was holding a hand to his bleeding
head, and Eileen was beside her husband, tears in her eyes and
her face stark white. Her eyes found mine and they widened,
her mouth opening to speak when a figure stepped into view.
Patterson.

I froze, fighting my initial instinct to flee. He looked the same
as the last time I saw him. Dressed all in black, he stood at six-
foot-two with long black hair, but it was longer now, down to
his shoulders. His lips twisted into a sick grin and merciless,
bottomless, black eyes that held no emotion locked onto me.
Once upon a time he'd appeared handsome to me, but now I
could see the monster lurking behind his mask.

My stomach dropped, not at the sight of him, but at the sight
of Mara standing shakily in front of him, her pale face a mask
of terror and a small blade pressed to her throat. I didn't miss
the gun in his other hand, his finger on the trigger

"I knew you'd figure it out," Patterson greeted.

"Selina," Mara wept, and Patterson pressed the blade tighter
until she flinched, and her voice was a strangled sob.

"Don't move, sweetheart. Don't speak," I told her, hoping my
voice was soothing.

"I have to say, it's quite a surprise that it took this long for you
to give in. But I should have known the safety of others was
what would bring you back to me, especially the little runt's,"

Patterson continued, his disdain for children written across his fierce features.

"Just let her go, and I'll go with you. Don't hurt her," I whispered, my mind scrambling for a way to get Mara out of this without further injury or trauma.

"You expect me to believe you'll stay this time?" he sneered, raising his gun to aim it at me, his blade still on Mara.

"Yes, because I will give you my word. You know how to hurt me now, more than just physically. I won't risk Mara or her family getting hurt by leaving you, because I know you'll hunt them down if I try," I answered, deciding honesty was best here.

His dark eyes searched my face, fathomless. I watched as his gaze tracked from me to behind me, and his satisfied smirk had me turning back a little to see Callan and his group behind me, their guns raised and leveled at Patterson.

"Daddy," Mara cried, and Patterson's blade pressed tighter into her so that she cried out. I took a half step forward before his eyes rested on me again, his head tilted to the side slightly, his gun never wavering.

"One wrong move, Selina, and I cut her throat. This knife is awfully sharp, as I'm sure you remember. Wouldn't want any accidents now, would we?" he taunted.

"Let her go," Callan growled beside me, the sound of his voice so deep and angry had the hairs on my arms and neck standing on end.

"Sure, since you asked," Patterson quipped.

"What do you want?" Cohen asked, his voice just as full of anger.

"I would have thought that was obvious. Did they really let someone so stupid into the Navy while they kicked me out?" Patterson answered, shaking his head in mock dismay.

"You're right… You are smart. The way you rigged up the AK-47's, each with their own 100 round drum magazine with a machine of your own invention to send off shots at random intervals… that's genius. You set up two guns in different locations to give us the impression we were dealing with multiple people," Flynn agreed, his aim unwavering as he continued to point his gun at Patterson. I inwardly shook my head. I knew he would never work with anyone else, and he really was smart enough to invent his own machines to shoot the guns at random.

"And you can hack into anything, including the security in a safe room," Parker added.

"Flattery won't make me any more inclined to work with you. If you hadn't guessed, hostage negotiation techniques don't work on someone like me," Patterson interceded, his shrewd eyes scanning over the soldiers.

"I'll go with you. Just let Mara go," I cut in quickly.

"This girl is my ticket out of here. How about you come with us? We'll be one happy family. I'm sure she'd like that. I could hear her in the safe room while I was hacking the code to break in as she told her grandparents all about how she was going to ask her daddy if you could be her mommy," Patterson replied, his delight in my pain obvious. A sharp pain stabbed at my chest, and I shook my head, needing to concentrate on Mara's safety and not how much I wanted to be her mother and how out of my reach that dream was.

"Hold onto her until we get to the car, fine. They won't risk shooting you in case they hit Mara," I advised.

"Selina," Callan warned but I ignored him.

"I don't think you really want to come back with me," Patterson pointed out coolly.

"No, I don't. But that's how you want me," I reminded. His

dark eyes glittered, and I edged forward again, bringing out the little knife. Callan made a sound of protest, but again, I ignored him.

"Come on, Patterson, you remember what it was like, don't you?" I coerced, dropping my voice an octave, allowing it to capture his attention. I raised the small blade slightly so his eyes snapped to it, and he watched with avid interest as I brought it to my inner forearm.

"You remember what it was like to take a blade to me, don't you?" I asked, slowly dragging it along my skin from my elbow to my wrist, wincing and biting my lip as blood dripped down my hand. It wasn't a deep cut, but it was more than enough to get his attention. I watched the blade pressing against Mara eased away ever so slightly as he became transfixed with my pain, my blood.

"What about the flogger? Or the whip you modified? Think about the toys you created to hurt me and never leave a permanent mark so that no-one was any the wiser. Remember what it was like to see me cry, beg, to scream. Remember my screams, Patterson?" I pressed, wanting to vomit at the memories, but it was distracting him. I could hear a sharp intake of breath behind me and a whispered curse, but otherwise everyone remained silent.

Patterson blinked once, then twice, as if coming back to himself. His dark eyes were no longer empty but filled with lust.

"You're going to step forward and take the girl. I will keep my gun on you. If anyone tries anything stupid, I kill you both," Patterson decided, his gaze swinging to the men around me, any lust or heat in his eyes evaporating so that nothing remained but that cold emptiness.

"Selina," Callan snapped again. I paused and took a moment to look back at him.

"We spoke about this in the forest, Callan. About what to do if it came down to a decision between Mara or me. Remember what I said. This isn't your decision, it is mine, you're just doing as I asked," I explained. His face was a mixture of rage, helplessness, and regret.

I turned back to Patterson, and he nodded for me to come closer. I made sure to keep my movements slow and precise, and I dropped the knife before I reached them. Mara's blue eyes were filled with tears and her little lips were trembling as she tried to hold back her cries.

"Hey, buttercup, it's going to be okay," I assured breathlessly as Patterson moved the blade from Mara to me. I winced when the blade nicked the skin at my neck, and carefully took Mara in my arms. The relief I felt at holding her was enormous, and I had to consciously stiffen my knees to prevent myself from collapsing. She was going to be okay. Her tiny arms wrapped around me so tight, and she buried her face against my shoulder, her quiet sobs making her shake.

Patterson swapped his blade for the and pressed it hard against my back between my shoulder blades. A gun like that, at this close range, the bullet would go through me and into Mara. I flicked a glance at Callan whose face was pale but tight, his jaw working and his eyes burning. His gaze met mine and softened slightly.

"I've got her," I whispered and drew in a steadying breath. "You're all going to back out of this hallway and into the kitchen. Selina and I are going to walk outside and to one of the cars—thanks for leaving the keys in them, by the way. If everyone does as they're told, we'll drop little Mara off at the base of the mountain and be gone before any of you reach her," Patterson instructed.

"No," I snapped, and winced when the gun pressed harder into my spine. "The deal was to leave Mara here," I reminded. "And I would be stupid to weaken my supply of bargaining chips. They won't risk running us off the road on these trails if we have the little welp in the car. They're going to give us a fifteen-minute head start, and if I see headlights in the rearview mirror, I'll shoot the girl," Patterson warned.

"Then you would have lost your protection."

"Ah, but none of you will risk her life on the off-chance of finding me," he reminded. I gritted my teeth and glanced at Callan and the guys. He was right, and we had no choice. None of them could open fire without risking mine or Mara's life. Patterson was planted firmly behind us, keeping low so as not to provide a clear shot. And if they took a shot and missed, Patterson could easily pull the trigger and kill one or both of his hostages.

"Move," Patterson ordered the group. After a long, tense moment, the soldiers began to slowly backtrack up the hall, weapons still pointed and ready. Patterson slammed the safe room door closed so that he had no one at his back and we very slowly started moving down the hallway. My ankle throbbed and screamed at me, but it was easy to ignore when my heart was pounding so hard. I had to find a way to get Mara out of this. Patterson would never keep his word and would either kill Mara and leave her at the bottom of the hill as a final *fuck you* to the military, or he'd take her with us and hurt her like he did me.

I wouldn't risk either option. My mind worked quickly as we edged out of the hallway and the guys backed into the kitchen as they were ordered. Patterson gripped my shoulder tightly and angled me towards the large sliding doors to the patio. My gaze clung to Callan as the muscle in his jaw worked and eyes swung between me and Mara.

Everywhere was dark. The moon was bright tonight, allowing for some light so that no one tripped. The sliding doors were open, and the cooler breeze washed over us and caused me to shiver.

"Daddy," Mara whimpered against my neck.

"Daddy will be fine, Mara," I promised, squeezing her hard. "And so will you."

We were headed for the stairs now, and Callan took a half step forward but was held back by Cohen when Patterson dug the gun hard enough into my spine to make me gasp in pain.

"You don't want to test me, soldier boy," Patterson warned in a deadly voice. Callan's blue eyes met mine again, and I gave the smallest of nods. I hope he understood, I hope he knew that I wouldn't let anything more happen to his little girl.

"Be brave, buttercup," I whispered in her ear, barely moving my lips, my voice barely detectable. Mara squeezed me again and I walked carefully down the stairs and kept my steps even and unhurried as Patterson directed us towards a car. I was extra careful to watch where I was walking in the dark, not wanting to fall with Mara in my arms or give Patterson any reason to think I was trying to escape or distract him.

"Get in first and climb over to the passenger's seat," Patterson ordered. It took some maneuvering, but I did as he ordered and found myself sitting with Mara on my lap as Patterson carefully climbed in. I glanced at the door handle and saw my door was unlocked. There was nothing but grass and dirt beside the car. It wouldn't be soft, but it was better than what was going to happen.

"I love you, buttercup. I would have been honored to be your mommy," I said to her again, feeling tears sting my eyes and clog my throat, but I did not let them fall. There was no time.

"Selina?" Mara questioned worriedly with tear-filled blue eyes, so much like her father's.

Patterson slammed his door closed and started the car. It was now or never.

"I'm sorry," I apologized tearfully before I kissed her face and as Patterson put the car into drive and pressed on the accelerator, I threw open my door and shoved Mara out of it. I heard her hit the ground hard, her little cry of alarm and pain tore at me. Patterson snarled at me and slammed the gun against my head. Pain and dizziness washed over me, and I barely registered as he leaned over me to slam my door closed before he sent us flying out of the long dirt driveway.

I blinked, hoping to see Mara in the side mirror and was glad to see Callan's taller silhouette scooping her up, flanked by his team, his brothers. Relief coursed through me, but it was short-lived as Patterson sent us flying around a corner, slamming me against the door and cracking my head against the window.

"Fucking stupid bitch!" Patterson snapped. "She was our leverage, our way out. They're not going to wait now. They'll risk your life to prove they never let an enemy get by them," he continued, spittle flying as he snarled and swore, spinning the steering wheel this way and that as he navigated the sharp switchback roads down the mountain. The headlights of the car were bright enough to light our way, but it was still hard to see every sharp bend in the dark. I was dizzy and struggled to see straight.

Mara was okay. Callan had her back now, and while I could never make up for the trauma that little girl had suffered, at least she was alive. Callan and his family would make sure she got through it and got any help she needed.

But now that she was safe, I had to look after myself, even if that meant no longer existing. I would never willingly put myself back in Patterson's hands if there was no need to. Mara was safe now, and I could use this opportunity to take him out too. I buckled my seatbelt as he sent us skidding precariously close to another edge before regaining control and continuing down the road. The rain we'd had the other night made the roads less safe and harder for the tires to grip to. This was the best chance I'd ever have. Patterson was always cool, calm, and collected. He had plans and escape routes and contingencies. He was always in charge… except for now. I'd never seen him so out of control, and I wasn't sure I'd ever get the chance again.

Sucking in another breath as my head pounded and my eyes struggled to focus, I glanced down at the hand break. We were coming up on another turn now. This was going to hurt, and knowing how steep these mountain sides were… I wasn't counting on surviving. In fact, I was aiming not to. Hopefully it wouldn't take long to die, but if it did, it was still preferable to being trapped with Patterson again.

I licked my lips as Patterson snarled another insult my way and leaned closer to him. Again, timing was everything. I waited as I felt the car lurch to the side as he spun us recklessly around another corner before I released his seatbelt. I caught the way his expression bled from confused to shocked and then to angry in the span of a second before I reefed up the handbrake, using my other hand to swipe hard at the side of his face, dragging my nails down his temple and cheek to distract him. I heard the crunch of tires as we spun, the handbrake snapped and gave way. Patterson's loud shout of pain rang in my ears as his head slammed forward into the dash, a sickening crunch of bones and splatter of blood. I closed my eyes as we spun out and then for one heart-stopping moment, we were airborne.

I opened my eyes in time to see us headed right for a thicket of bushes before the car landed hard. I was lifted out of my seat when the car left the ground, the back of my head smashed into the roof of the car before my seatbelt yanked me back into my seat and I was almost immediately thrown forward again as the car plowed into the bushes and smaller trees. The seatbelt caught me once more, digging hard into my ribs and collarbone, squeezing the air from my lungs, pain searing through me. The car tipped onto its side and slammed into the ground, leaving me hanging in my seat, Patterson's door pressed into the ground. I couldn't hear anything through the blood rushing in my ears and my heartbeat pounding so hard I was sure the entire mountainside could hear it.

And then... silence.

Noise suddenly came back to me, and my own breath sounded too sharp, too loud, too fast. A hissing from the motor or the radiator spread through the otherwise silent forest, and the smell of oil, smoke, blood, and burnt rubber permeated the air. I blinked, my vision blurry, my body aching, and turned my head slightly to look at Patterson.

I didn't need to touch him to see that he was dead. His eyes were frozen open, blood smeared half of his face, and his neck was bent at an unnatural angle.

Awareness was fading in and out, and my body felt too heavy to move. I was one giant, throbbing, aching bruise, and I didn't want to feel it anymore. Darkness was crowding close when the sound of cars reached me, sirens somewhere far off. Help was coming.

Relief washed over me, but I wondered if it would be too late. Someone called my name, and I frowned. There it was again, but it was so far away, and darkness kept crowding me, tempting me with the numb void that awaited. There was movement beside me, the car rocked. There was that voice again, but it was too hard to open my eyes and see who it was.

Chapter Thirteen

CALLAN

"Callan, wait!" Cohen shouted behind me, but I was already out of his reach and out the sliding door. That psycho had my baby girl. He had Selina. Like fuck I was giving him a fifteen-minute head start.

I leapt from the porch and reached the bottom of the stairs, searching the darkness when I saw the passenger's side door of the car open, and Mara was shoved out of it. The car shot off out of the driveway and Mara hit the ground hard, her cry of pain wrenching through me.

"Mara!" I shouted, and I was at her side in an instant. I'd moved so fast, it felt like I'd blinked and was at her side. "Daddy!" she sobbed, raising her arms. I swept her up immediately, and her tiny body shuddered against me as she broke down in tears. I glanced at the quickly disappearing car to see the passenger's door slam closed—Patterson's arm—as the car flew recklessly down the dirt roads to disappear out of sight.

Selina.

She saved Mara, she'd managed to do what she could to get my baby out of danger, even knowing it would leave her open to an attack.

Jason, Flynn, Cohen, followed by West came barreling down the driveway after me, stopping to look at Mara and make sure she was okay.

"D-daddy," Mara sobbed, pulling back to look at me. Her skin was unnaturally pale in the moonlight, her blue eyes filled with tears and shock. I could see the little red cuts on her throat from the blade Patterson had held to it, and my vision grew red with rage. I looked back at the now empty driveway, my every instinct screaming at me to go after the car, to save Selina, to put a bullet in that fucking psycho's head. But I had my daughter to look after. She was hurt and traumatized, and I couldn't just abandon her...

"I'm here, baby," I whispered, barely pulling myself under control. I glanced up at the sound of Eileen calling Mara's name, and saw her and Lyle stagger towards us, Parker behind them. The lights were back on now, the floodlights lighting up the entire backyard. Parker had to have let them out of the safe room and turned the power back on. Lyle had blood trickling down the side of his head, and he looked pale and a little unsteady on his feet, but nothing was stopping him from getting to us to see Mara.

"She's okay," I called out and watched as Eileen's legs gave out in relief a few feet from us. Lyle slid to his knees beside her and wrapped an arm around her shaking shoulders.

"Daddy," Mara sobbed again, tugging at my shirt.

"What is it, baby?"

"Selina... he's going to hurt Selina. You have to help her," she cried, her little voice ravaged with pain.

"Baby..."

"Please, Daddy. She loves me, she calls me buttercup like her daddy called her. She's so scared and that man is going to hurt her. Please, Daddy, I love her," she cried, her face distraught.

"We've got her, Callan. I've already called the Sheriff's station and they're on their way with an ambulance. Eileen will help me look Mara over for injuries. Go save her," Parker told me, and I could see how badly Mara's desperation affected him. I peered around at my brothers to see similar looks on their faces. They were all soldiers too, and we didn't let innocents get hurt when we could stop it.

"I love you, baby girl."

Mara nodded and I kissed her quickly before handing her over to Parker, my heart pounding hard in my chest at the thought of leaving her behind. But they were right, Selina needed us right now... needed me. Like hell I was letting that psychotic asshole have her.

"Let's go," I clenched out. Jason and Cohen nodded, flanking me on either side, West and Flynn at our backs. I jumped into the driver's seat of Flynn's SUV and the guys all piled in with me, checking their weapons. I didn't hesitate another second. As soon as the doors were closed, we skidded down the dirt road. My heart was pounding and aching at the thought of what could happen to Selina. These roads were treacherous at the best of times, but to drive them as recklessly as Patterson had so soon after a rainstorm and in the dark was suicidal. They could die out here. And what if they didn't? Patterson was incredibly smart and could hack anything. He could give them new identities and money anywhere in the world and we'd never find them again.

"You remember what it was like to take a blade to me, don't you?" Selina's whispered words floated back to me, and my stomach clenched hard as I recalled the way she cut her arm, the way Patterson's gaze became transfixed, enamored, totally zoned in on the sight of her blood and the pain on her face. He was a true sadist and couldn't resist watching her in pain.

"Remember what it was like to see me cry, beg, to scream. Remember my screams, Patterson?"

Fuck. She'd been through all that before and was going to do it again to save my daughter.

I took the sharp corners as fast as I dared, reminding myself that we were no good to anyone dead.

"Did she tell you how bad this guy was?" West asked.

"Briefly. We didn't have time to get into much detail," I gritted out.

"Fuck, man… The things she was saying back there about what he used to do to her…"

Cohen trailed off.

"Let's put this fucker down, yeah?" Jason suggested, his voice tight. I glanced at him in the rearview mirror and his face was a mask of anger and disgust.

There was a sound of unanimous agreement.

"There!" Flynn called, and I slowed at the sight of deep skid marks, ones different to the others we'd seen so far. These ones were deeper, wilder… out of control. It didn't take us long to see the smoke and the faded beam of light from headlights. I'd barely stopped the car before I was out and running down the hill, calling Selina's name. I used the torch on my gun to light my way, but the beam of light was weak in this kind of darkness and barely lit two feet in front of me.

Don't let her be dead. Please, don't let me lose her too.

"Selina!" I shouted as I shoved past several bushes and finally caught sight of the smashed-up car below, turned on its side, smoke rising from the hood.

"Fuck," Cohen swore from behind me. I could hear sirens in the distance and hoped like fuck we weren't too late.

I started for the car again, almost stumbling over branches and roots as I ran for the car calling her name. I slammed into it as I reached it, losing my footing on the slippery ground.

"Selina!" I shouted, lifting myself onto the car to look inside. My breath caught at the sight of Selina, held in place by her seatbelt. Blood coated the side of her face from a wound on her head, and her eyes were fluttering as if she were fighting unconsciousness.

"Selina, I'm here." I reached in to stroke her face, careful where I touched. I wanted to drag her from the car, but I knew it was dangerous. I didn't want to risk causing her further injury when there was an ambulance on its way.

She made a soft sound of distress, and I slid my hand down her arm to take one of hers. The knuckles were red and bloody.

"Selina, wake up, spitfire. I'm here, stay with me," I urged as the car rocked gently and I glanced up to see Cohen come up too. I looked past Selina to Patterson, and it was obvious from here that he was dead. I could be happy about that later, but my concern for Selina was too great right now.

"Callan?" she murmured, her lips barely moving.

"I'm here, baby. Stay with me, spitfire, stay awake. Help is on the way," I replied, hope flaring inside me now that she was speaking.

"I... will try... top-shelf," she muttered brokenly. A small, relieved laugh escaped me, and I blinked back the burning in my eyes. I hadn't cried since Mara was born and I'd lost Lina.

"You saved my baby-girl, thank you," I whispered brokenly. Selina frowned and swallowed hard, the effort to stay awake was obviously wearing on her. "Cohen, find out how far the ambulance is and run back to tell them what they're looking at, so they don't have to go back for equipment," I ordered. Cohen nodded and was gone just as quickly.

"Is M-Mara... okay? Had to... push her. Didn't w-wanna... hurt her," Selina rasped, her breathing heavier and her words slurring.

"She's okay, she's going to be fine," I assured quickly, squeezing her hand.

"Crashed the car... d-didn't wanna go back... with him," she mumbled, her breath hitching, and a pained expression tightened her face.

"You crashed the car?" I asked, wanting to keep her talking.

"Mmm… un-unbuckled his belt. Handbrake… skidded," Selina mumbled again, but I understood. My heart clenched at the thought of what she did to avoid going through hell with that maniac again. She'd expected to die… probably planned to.

"He's dead now. He can't hurt you," I promised.

"S-sorry… for all… this… Cal…" She trailed off again, the stretches between her words getting longer and longer. She hadn't even opened her eyes yet, too out of it. She hadn't moved either, no more than a little shake of her head. Fuck… *fuck!*

I tried to quell the panic rising in my chest, but my training wasn't helping this time. I heard voices further away and knew Cohen had to be back with help.

"Hang on, Selina. Help is here."

Selina didn't respond this time, and I froze at the sight of her face going slack.

"Selina?"

Nothing.

"Selina!" I shouted, barely refraining from shaking her.

"Someone get some fucking help down here!" I roared up the mountain, desperation shredding at my composure as I watched Selina slide further away from me.

Not again… please.

~

SELINA

Five Weeks Later

"So as soon as your doctor signs off, you can be discharged today," Nurse Marriot explained with a bright smile. She was one of my favorite nurses here, and I'd gotten to know a couple of them during my stay.

"Do you want me to call one of those fine men to come and pick you up?" she asked with a wink. I smiled and shook my head.

"No, thank you. I'll just take a cab," I replied. She frowned slightly, questions in her eyes, but I didn't want to answer them.

"Could I trouble you for some more water?" I asked instead. She gave me a gentle, knowing smile, and nodded.

"Of course, honey. Be right back," she answered and left on silent feet.

I'd been in hospital for five weeks, but I'd only been conscious for a week of it. A month spent in a medically induced coma due to brain trauma. My brain had swelled, and they'd been worried about spinal damage, memory loss, and potential brain damage. In addition to that, there had been several lacerations, three fractured ribs, bone bruising on my chest, shoulders, and hips from where the belt had kept me in my seat. I had *so* many bruises to start with, as well as the cut on my arm and the sprained ankle. Thankfully I'd been asleep for most of the recovery time, so now I was just a little achy but could move fine. Someone *up there*—I was going to say my father—had protected me from worse and permanent injuries.

At first, I hadn't remembered anything beyond meeting Cohen in the forest when I'd been in the river. But soon, everything came back, and I was wracked with guilt. Seriously... how was I ever meant to make any of this up to Callan or Mara? In the end, I just figured it was better to leave quietly so they could put all this behind them. They'd been to see me, of course. Nurse Marriot had told me he'd been by my bed for hours at a time for that first month—all the guys had, even Lyle and Eileen. They hadn't wanted me to wake up alone. Knowing that, it should have made me feel better about everything. They cared enough that they didn't want me to wake up alone. But how could they forgive me, how could I forgive myself for bringing this into their lives?

Mara was doing okay. The first time she'd come to visit me, she hadn't moved off my bed where she was plastered to my side. She told me all about her nightmares and how scared she'd been that night, but how I'd told her to be brave, so she tried her hardest not to be scared.

Callan told me he had her in therapy to help, and that she'd started school and had already made friends. I was sad I'd missed her first day, but really... I wasn't going to be around much longer anyway.

The guys had all come to see me too, and I really wished I could stay and get to know them better. They were a good bunch—flirty, funny, and so kind. They all tried to tell me nothing was my fault, but how could they really believe that? Thankfully, none of them had been hurt in the crossfire, so that was a relief.

Lyle and Eileen had come to see me a few times, happy that I was awake. They constantly thanked me for saving Mara, for putting myself in that situation to save her, but I couldn't accept their thanks and always changed the subject. The bottom line was; none of them would have had to go through this trauma if I hadn't dragged the issue along with me. Anything I did that they considered brave was the bare minimum of what I should have done to correct the mistake I made by letting them help me in the first place.

The police had been to see me as well. Callan and everyone else had given their statements, but they still needed to hear it from me. I told them everything, and they explained that Patterson had died almost instantly when his head hit the dash as it snapped his neck. I didn't care that he hadn't suffered like he'd made me suffer, I was just glad he was gone and couldn't hurt anyone again.

Thankfully, I wasn't in any trouble for the actions I took, and they had wrapped everything up and closed the report.

Nurse Marriot came back fifteen minutes later with some more water and discharge papers.

"Are you sure you don't want me to call someone?" she asked and I nodded.

"Thank you, Nurse Marriot, but I'm okay. I have to get home and get packing," I explained.

"You're leaving?"

"Yeah, it's time I move on," I replied, pulling my jacket on, relishing in not feeling any more pain.

"But I thought... well... with how that Callan guy looked at you and how close you and that little Mara are... I thought you'd be staying?"

I avoided her eyes as I zipped up my jacket and shrugged.

"It's better this way," I answered softly. Being such a small town, everyone knew what had happened, so I didn't need to explain anything to her.

"For what it's worth... I think you're making a mistake," she warned.

"I know," I said with a small smile. She huffed impatiently and shook her head.

"I'll call you that cab. Please, take it easy?"

I leaned forward and hugged her, stunning her temporarily until she hugged me back. When she pulled back, she patted my hand and then left. I grabbed my bag that the guys brought for me—complete with my dad's shirt—and took another look around. There was nothing else here for me.

An hour later, I was at home and surveying my apartment. I hadn't been here all that long, so I didn't have a lot. The furniture could all stay, I didn't need to take it with me, and what I had to take was mostly still packed. I hadn't fully unpacked my things in three years thanks to Patterson.

First, a shower to wash away the smell of the hospital, then I could get to work packing up. I'd sleep here tonight and leave in the morning.

Chapter Fourteen

CALLAN

I brushed a hand nervously over my hair as I strode down the hospital corridor. I'd left Mara with her grandparents, wanting to speak to Selina in private. There was a lot we hadn't been able to talk about over the last week while Mara and other visitors had been there. Mostly, I was just overwhelmingly grateful that she hadn't suffered any lasting injuries. The doctors all said that it was a miracle that she wasn't more wounded, and that she came out of it with temporary damages.

Mara said it was her mama and Selina's daddy who worked together to protect her. I was inclined to agree.

Watching her go slack in that car and stop responding, I was terrified she'd died right in front of me. Thankfully, the paramedics around here were well versed in getting injured parties from cars perched as precariously as hers had been. With the mountains being as they were, they had experience in pulling survivors out without causing further damage.

I wanted Selina. I'd spent an entire month at her bedside, hoping she'd get better, and thinking about what I'd say when she was—*if* she was. Mostly, I thought about those three days in the forest and how they'd changed me completely. Who knew I had to get lost on my own mountain to find the woman I was meant to spend my life with?

I reached Selina's room and frowned when her bed was empty, and all her belongings were gone. I double-checked the room number, but it was the same one.

"Uh, excuse me," I called out to a nurse who had looked after Selina a lot.

"Oh, Mr. Callan," she greeted. I grinned.

"Just Callan is fine. Uh, where is Selina? Did they move her?" I asked. Her face fell for a moment, and she shook her head.

"I'm sorry. No, Selina was discharged this morning," she explained. I stilled and frowned harder.

"What do you mean she was discharged? How? She can't be alone right now," I demanded. The nurse sighed and waved me over to a desk where she shuffled through some files and shook her head.

"I asked her if I could call anyone, and she said no. I even mentioned you and Mara by name, but she said it was better this way. She, uh…" she trailed off, looking a little guilty.

"What? Just tell me," I begged quietly.

"She's leaving," she said quickly. A beat passed, and then another.

"What do you mean?"

"I mean, she wanted to go home and pack because she said she's leaving town. I told her I thought it was a bad idea, but she was determined that it was what's best. I think she's feeling guilty about everything," the nurse continued. My head spun and I shook my head. No, she couldn't leave, not now.

"Can you tell me her address? I really need to speak to her." The nurse smiled sympathetically and shook her head. "I'm sorry, that's private information."

"There has to be something. I can't lose her, not now, I just got her back," I groaned, running my fingers through my hair in agitation. The nurse studied me for a good long moment and looked carefully around before flipping through her folders.

"I'm sorry, Callan, there's really nothing I can do. Patient information is confidential," she said, waving a folder at me before placing it open—face up—on the desk. "Now, I have to make a quick call over here. Shouldn't take me more than twenty seconds. I'm sorry, Callan. Good luck," she said. I frowned and her eyes shifted to the file briefly before she winked and turned her back to make a call.

My breath caught, and I quickly searched around before shuffling around the desk to stare down at the paperwork. I scanned it, glancing over her name and other information before I found her address. Memorizing it, I closed the file and strode away from the desk, making a mental note to send the nurse some flowers if this worked.

I hurried out of the hospital and jogged to my car, hoping she hadn't gone already. It was just after lunch, but I had a feeling that my woman moved quickly. I took a second to try and remember where her street was located before I threw my truck into drive and headed in her direction. She couldn't leave before I at least had a chance to say my piece, to ask her to stay. Mara would never forgive me if I didn't at least ask, and I would hate myself for being a coward.

It only took me ten minutes to reach her street, and I slowed down until I found her number. She had a small apartment wedged between three others and it was up a few stairs. A car was in the driveway, and I had to assume it was hers.

Sucking in a deep breath, I exited my truck and locked it before jogging up her stairs. This was it. I had to lay it all out for her before she left, make her see reason, and remind her that we had something. I had to tell her how watching her drive away with that psycho had hurt in a way I hadn't known was possible, that it had terrified me to know what she could be destined for. It had warmed me to know she had done it to save my daughter, and her strength left me in awe of her. I had to hope she remembered how it was when we were together and none of this guilt was between us. We fit; it was as easy as breathing. I hadn't thought I'd find another woman who fit me as well as my wife had, but here she was, and she was perfect for Mara too.

Not giving myself any more time, I rapped on the door and waited.

"Coming!" her voice called from inside, and relief hit me. She was still here, it wasn't someone else's car. I waited impatiently for what was probably only a few seconds but felt like minutes. The locks clicked and I opened my mouth to start talking the second the door opened, but stopped dead, all the air in my lungs evaporating at the sight of her in nothing but a white towel, her hair damp down her back, her body still glistening with water.

"Callan," she gasped, and the way she said my name sent me over the edge. I stepped in close, slid my hand around her waist and hauled her up against me before I brought my mouth crashing down on hers. I caught her gasp of surprise and slid my tongue into her mouth before I tangled my other hand in her hair and tugged gently on the damp strands as I kissed her for all I was worth. It didn't take her long to kiss me back, and I was more than relieved that she wasn't pushing me away and putting space between us. I backed her up into her apartment and kicked the door closed behind me, never once lifting my head from hers. Her hands were bunched in the front of my shirt, her body moving restlessly against mine, a small sound of pleasure coming from her throat.

"Never answer the door dressed like this again," I murmured against her mouth before I kissed her hard again. The thought of anyone else seeing her like this was enough to drive me mad.

"Okay," she whispered as I backed her up against the wall and she tugged at my shirt, lifting it. I grabbed the material at the back of my neck and pulled it up over my head before tossing it aside. There was a second of her gaping at me before I kissed her again. Her fingers traced my heated skin and I groaned, wanting more. I kicked off my shoes and her hands went to my belt where she hurriedly unbuckled it before unzipping my jeans.

Fuck, yes.

I tugged at her towel, and she gasped when it fell and pooled at her feet. I slid my hands down her side to her backside and I lifted. She took the hint and let me lift her up, wrapping her legs around my hips and her arms around my waist.

"Bedroom?" I questioned without taking my lips from hers.

"Last door at the end of the hall."

I walked blindly, kissing her like I'd die if I stopped and kicked the already ajar door open to stumble inside. I sat her carefully on the edge of the queen-sized bed and leaned over her, forcing her to lie backwards.

"Selina," I said with a small pant, lifting my head to look down at her. Dark eyes stared heatedly up at me, her cheeks pink and lips swollen. "I need you to know something," I began, and she shook her head. I silenced her with another kiss and then looked down at her again. "I do not blame you for anything that happened. Patterson was psychotic and had attached himself to you. If it wasn't me and Mara, it would have been someone else you became involved with, and they may not have been as prepared or as well off as we were. Mara is okay, and thriving, and she's moving on with her life. I would like to do the same thing, but my stubborn, pain in the ass woman keeps trying to use her guilt to put a block between us," I told her firmly.

"But... everything that happened. Your home, your in-laws, Mara—"

"Are all fine. The house can be repaired, Mara's grandparents are well and truly over it and are nothing but grateful for what you did and how strong and smart you were. The guys have nothing but high praises to sing about you. Mara wants you to move in and be with us forever. No one is blaming you for anything," I assured. Her dark eyes glittered with unshed tears, and I kissed each eyelid before trailing light kisses back to her mouth.

"And you?"

"I'm pissed as hell," I answered. She stilled beneath me, her eyes wide and worried. "I'm pissed because I thought we had a deal. When we were in the forest and you laid everything out in painful detail and said that if Patterson makes a move and it's a choice between you and Mara, that I was to get Mara out, that it was what you wanted... you didn't stick to your end of the deal."

"What do you mean?"

"I mean," I sighed and kicked off my jeans before I dragged her further up the bed and leaned over her again, caging her in. "The deal was, that I run and get Mara to safety, but that you fight any way you can, and I'll come back for you. I just needed you to hold on."

Confusion still clouded her eyes and I smiled gently and kissed her again.

"You didn't give me time to find you, Selina. You tried to run the car off the road with the intention of killing yourself and him so that you didn't end up back in his hands. You didn't fight and give me time to get to you, you just tried to end things."

Her eyes glistened, and she shook her head. "I knew Patterson well. I knew what he was capable of… I didn't want to risk that hell when I wasn't sure you'd ever be able to find me."

"I know," I whispered. "But I'm hoping in the future, you'll have more faith in me and my ability to keep my word. I don't make promises I can't keep."

"The future?"

"Yes." I smiled. "The future in which I am hoping you will let me make love to you. Again, and again."

Her smile softened as I stroked her cheek and leaned down to kiss her. She wrapped her arms around my neck as I deepened the kiss and she rocked against me. A moan escaped me, and she smirked against my lips before doing it again. It didn't take long before the heat between us built up once more and I kissed down her throat to her breasts where I sucked on each nipple, drawing cries of ecstasy from her. My mouth watered at the idea of tasting her again, and I decided to allow myself that luxury as I moved between her legs.

"Callan, you don't have—oh, yes!" she cried, her back arching and her hips moving with my mouth. I ate her like she was my last meal, and I was starving. When she was on the brink, I slid two fingers inside her and crooked them, stroking her, winding her tighter and tighter until she came, crying my name in a hoarse voice. The sound of her coming, crying my name because of what I was doing to her made my dick weep. She shook hard and swore quietly, her breathing labored and choppy. I raised my head to look down at her and she grinned.

"How sore are you?" I asked, remembering her injuries. She shook her head, wound her legs around my hips, and heaved up. I ended up on my back with her on top and she laughed gently.

"Not enough to stop this," she assured breathlessly.

"Are you sure?" My hands stroked her hips as she rocked against my hard length.

"Don't ask stupid questions."

I smiled back and groaned as she continued her torturous grinding, feeling her slick heat coat my aching cock. Fuck, I wanted to be inside her already, but watching her in control, watching her set the pace was too much to pass up. I cupped her breasts and tweaked her sensitive nipples and she gasped and moaned.

"Selina," I gritted out. If she kept this up much longer, I was going to come before we even got started.

"Impatient much?" She laughed breathlessly.

"For you? Fuck yes."

The little minx laughed low and then paused

"I don't have any condoms," she whispered, her eyes wide with dread.

"Grab my jeans," I ordered. I watched as she scurried naked to my jeans and tugged out my wallet. She hurriedly picked out the condom—one of three—and tore it open.

"Here, let me," I offered but she smiled cheekily and shook her head. Raising an eyebrow, I crossed my arms behind my head and watched her shuffle up to me on her knees, her body a work of art. I bit back a groan as she slid the condom onto my cock that was standing at attention, and she smirked triumphantly.

"Ride me, Selina," I ordered, desperate for her now. If she didn't take me inside her soon, I was going to take over, and she was having so much fun. Biting her lower lip, Selina edged up over me until she sat with a leg on either side. I kept my hands where they were behind my head as she took my cock in her hand and pressed me to her entrance. Slowly, her eyes locked with mine, she slid down over me, her mouth opening in a silent moan, her eyes closing in pleasure. I gritted my teeth and lifted my hips at the scorching heat of her, so wet and tight it was pleasure bordering on pain.

"Fuck." My breath hissed out between my teeth. Selina moved slowly, rocking, sliding up and down on my length, and I couldn't take it anymore. Gripping her hips, I raised mine and thrust into her harder. She gasped and moaned, clenching tight around me. She began to rock faster, and I continued to thrust upwards as she lowered herself down. I wanted this to last forever, I wanted to take my time and draw this out, but it was too late. This time was going to be hard and dirty. Wrapping my arms around her, I spun us so that she was beneath me, and I thrust into her harder. Her nails dug into my back, and I groaned.

"Yes, Callan, please," she begged, her words breathy and desperate. I pushed her knees further up, drilling into her as hard and deep as I could go.

"Come on my cock, baby. I got you. Come for me," I encouraged, grinding against her as I thrusted, making sure to hit her clit every time. She whimpered, almost purred when I didn't let up, and I could feel her getting closer and closer. I was so close, barely holding back until she came first.

"Callan," she moaned.

"Come, Selina. Come for me, baby," I encouraged breathlessly, moving faster, shorter, the tingle in my spine starting.

"Yes, yes, God, yes!" Selina cried, her back arching and nails digging deep.

"Fuck!" I roared, feeling myself come hard inside her, my body shaking. A light behind my eyes blew, momentarily blinding me. My muscles felt like jelly, and I struggled not to collapse on top of her.

I don't know how much time passed before we were looking at each other, breathing slightly labored and grinning.

"Worth the wait?"

"Fuck yes," I groaned. She laughed and I pulled out of her reluctantly before I got up and dealt with the condom. When I came back, she was wrapped up in the sheet, sitting with her knees drawn up.

Silence hung between us for a moment, and I slid my briefs back on before taking a seat on the side of the bed, facing her.

"The nurse at the hospital said you're leaving town?"

Selina bit her lower lip and nodded slowly. "Yes."

"Do you really want to leave?"

"No."

"Then stay," I urged. A smile tugged at her lips, and she sighed.

"What if me staying here only makes things harder for Mara to move on?"

"You mean the little girl who has been begging me since the moment you opened your eyes to ask you to be her mommy, to move in with us and be my girlfriend? *That* Mara?" I asked. Selina's face flushed pink, and I caught her pleased smile. "She loves you, Selina." Her eyes shot to my face, and I nodded. "That night when I picked her up, she begged me to go after you, to look after you. She said she loves you and that you called her buttercup and that you were scared. I held her for less than a minute before she begged me to go after you. And every day since, the only thing she has been worried about is if you're going to wake up and not want to come live with us," I continued. Selina's eyes shone with unshed tears, and I slid in close to her and pulled her onto my lap so she sat astride me. She tried to cover up, but I yanked the blankets away and tipped her head up to meet my gaze.

"I want you to stay, Selina. I want *you*, and I want to see where this goes between us. We had a strong connection from the beginning, and I feel like we were meant to find you that day. You make me feel unlike anyone else, and I know that letting you go will be a massive mistake. I know being with me isn't simple, I come with an extra person and she's as permanent in my life as the sun and the moon. I've seen how you are with her, how much you already love her. You were going to sacrifice yourself for her that night, and that proves to me you love her. Selina... You belong with us, with Mara and me," I explained, watching the emotions chase across her face. I gave her a few minutes and wished I could read her mind and the thoughts she hid behind those brown eyes.

"Selina? What are you thinking?"

"Home," she whispered. I frowned. "Since my father died, I have been searching for a place that felt like home. I've been to a lot of places, but nowhere felt right. And then I realized that home wasn't just a place, but with people who made it so. I was just thinking that when I'm with you and Mara, I feel like I'm home," she explained softly, and a tear escaped her dark eyes. I wiped it away and felt hope burst in my chest, so powerful I hardly dared to breathe.

"So..." I trailed off.

"I want you, Callan. I want Mara, I want to see where this goes, and I want a life with the two of you," she explained shakily, her smile wide and tremulous.

"I need to hear you say the words, baby," I urged, still holding my breath.

"I'm staying," she agreed. I grinned as I slid my hands up into her hair and tugged her face closer to kiss her, pulling her tight against me. Nothing had tasted sweeter than that kiss. Like Selina said, kissing her was like coming home.

Epilogue

CALLAN

"The blue shirt, Daddy! Mama said it makes your eyes stand out," Mara reminded in exasperation. I chuckled and took my blue button-up off the hanger and slid it on, doing up the buttons. Mara was standing on the bed behind me and I ran a comb over my hair. Selina—or as Mara now called her, Mama—had an exhibit in the local art gallery tonight to show off some of her incredible nature shots. Six months ago, we'd gone back to the mountainside where we'd met a year ago and we'd waited there for two whole days so she could get the photo of the bird she'd tried to take a photo of when we met. Then we'd hiked around for another four days while she took photos of all of us and the view. It had been important for us to go camping again, especially to that spot, and help Mara through any lingering worries about camping in the woods. One of Selina's photos tonight was of Mara looking up into a sunset. The photo was close to her face and set in black and white, but it was so clear that the view of the mountains and stream were discernible in her bright eyes. It was my favorite of all the ones she'd taken.

To say Mara had been overjoyed a year ago at knowing Selina was staying in town and that we'd be seeing a lot more of her, would be an understatement. Within three months, Selina was living with us. Three months after that, Mara asked if she could call her Mommy. Not wanting Mara to forget about her birth mother, Selina suggested Mama instead. Mara had been more than happy with that, this way she had a mommy and a mama. As if I needed another reason to love that woman, she never let Mara forget her mother and encouraged us both to talk about her, to share memories and keep her alive in that way.

Tomorrow was our one-year anniversary, and we were planning to go away for the long weekend, just the two of us. But first, I had something to do. It had taken a lot of planning and convincing of the right people, but tonight I was going to propose. Mara had helped me to pick out the ring and was overjoyed at the idea of me and Selina getting married. I tugged the small box out of my pocket and peered down at it.

"Daddy! Put it away, Mama might see," Mara insisted urgently.

"Right, of course," I muttered and sucked in a deep breath.

"Are you nervous?" she asked. I still couldn't believe how grown up she was at only seven years old.

"A little," I admitted.

"Do you think she'll say no?"

"No." I answered, shaking my head. "I just hope I do it right."

"I know what to say when it's time. You'll do great, Daddy," she encouraged with a grin. I turned around and wrapped my arms around her tightly and Mara giggled when I tickled her. I loved this little girl so much.

"Are you two ready? We're going to be late if we don't hurry," Selina called, ducking her head into the bedroom and grinning at Mara's little giggles.

"Yes, Mara was just helping me with my hair." I winked.

"I like the shirt choice," Selina complimented with an appreciative look.

"I helped. Daddy was going to wear the black one, Mama." Mara outed me, rolling her eyes at the idea as she jumped from the bed and took Selina's hand.

"Well, I'm glad you were there to set him straight," Selina returned, grinning at me again before she led Mara out the door. I watched them both go, both dressed in beautiful red dresses, Mara's hair in braids while Selina wore hers out and curled.

I was a fucking lucky man.

~

SELINA

Nervous didn't even begin to cover what I was feeling.

This was the first time my work had been displayed in a public gallery, and I was worried it would all be a total flop. Callan had been amazing these last few months while I put everything together, and Mara was my shadow, my constant companion, and I loved her to bits. The night I was tucking her into bed, and she asked if she could call me Mommy was one of the happiest of my life. I'd explained it to Callan and burst into tears, my heart so full. I never wanted it to look like I was trying to replace her mother, so I'd asked her if Mama was acceptable, and she'd eagerly accepted. Callan was more than happy with the arrangement and reminded me often how much he loved me for letting Mara feel safe in wanting to know her birth mother. She was hungry for the details, and I encouraged her to ask questions and put out photos in her room.

Tonight, all the guys had shown up and I was so happy. Mara's grandparents were here too, and they had been nothing but accepting of mine and Callan's relationship and Mara calling me Mama. They'd seemed relieved, honestly, and happy for us.

I watched people mill about tonight, taking their time as they took in all the beautiful portraits around them. There were a lot of talented artists here tonight, and I was worried mine would not be up to their standard. After watching people look at my photos for a while, I'd moved on. It was too hard to watch, my stomach was in knots, and I couldn't stand the idea of seeing someone hate them. Yes, I knew art was subjective and not everyone would like my photos, but putting them up like this for people to look at and judge was a huge step for me.

I gripped the pendant around my neck and sent a little message to my dad, asking him to make tonight go smoothly and wonderful for me. Just having a part of him near went a long way to soothing my nerves.

"Mama!" Mara cried, pushing through the crowd. I spun at the alarm in her voice and watched her distraught face as she found me.

"Buttercup, what's wrong?"

"Something is wrong with one of your photos. The man is getting very upset saying it's stolen," Mara cried. Blood drained from my face, and I took her little hand. Stolen? How on earth could it have been stolen? I took all these photos myself in the mountains. Stomach churning, I weaved through the crowd with Mara until we got to our exhibit and came to a halt. Everyone was crowded around in a semicircle, facing my photos. All of Callan's brothers were there, grinning, as were Mara's grandparents. The air was expectant, excited, and I frowned.

"What's..." I trailed off, my attention shifting to my photos. But they weren't my photos. Well, they were, but not the ones I'd put up for public viewing.

The first photo was of me and Callan, an up-close image of us kissing, one I'd used a timer for. The second photo was of Callan, me, and Mara at the river. The third photo was of Callan and Mara dancing at Mara's seventh birthday. The fourth photo was of Mara and me placing a flower crown on her head. And the fifth photo was another one of me and Callan. No one could tell of course, it was our silhouettes as we stood waist-deep in the river, shirtless and pressed against one another, the moon coming up behind us.

Beneath each photo was a single word.

Selina. Will. You. Marry. Me?

I drew in a shaky breath, my eyes widening and pricking with tears as I slowly turned to see Callan step forward. His expression was one of deep devotion, his eyes shining with pride and love and his smile... Christ, that smile.

"Selina," he began and slowly dropped to one knee. "I never thought I'd find another woman I'd love so much in my life. I was prepared for Mara and me to face the world alone for as long as she needed me. That was until one fateful day when you literally fell into my lap," he began. There was a small chuckle from those who knew the story and I laughed too. "Our story may have started out intense and steeped in mystery and darkness, but we've faced off against those shadows together ever since. You have become a wonderful mother to our daughter, and I cannot express how much I love seeing you two together, how much you love her. It shines from within you whenever you look at her, and knowing it, seeing it, is a priceless gift," he continued. I wiped at a wayward tear and nodded, unable to speak. Callan slowly reached out and took my hand and I felt it shake slightly.

"I love you, Selina. I think I have loved you from the very first moment you called me a sasquatch, a yeti, and a mountain man," he continued. More scattered laughter and I bit my lip, remembering that day clearly.

"I don't know what I did to deserve you, but I'm grateful for whatever twist of fate that brought us together that day. Finding you was like finding home again. So, marry me, Selina. Be mine forever and I swear I'll spend the rest of my life making sure you never regret falling for a mountain man," Callan finished, holding out a beautiful ring with two sapphire hearts embedded in the white-gold band. I already knew those blue hearts represented Mara and Callan.

"Yes," I answered breathily, my voice breaking. "Yes, of course, yes!"

Callan grinned, his shoulders drooping in relief as applause and cheers broke out around us. Callan slipped the ring onto my finger and stood quickly, crushing his mouth to mine. I wrapped my arms around him and kissed him for all I was worth, my heart so full it felt like it was going to burst.

"I love you, Selina," he murmured, staring down at me with eyes so full of love. I stroked his trimmed beard and grinned.

"I love you, mountain man." Callan chuckled and kissed me again, but we were interrupted with a small tugging at our side. We pulled apart and I grinned down at Mara.

"I knew you'd say yes!" She cried and hugged me. We both wrapped our arms around her, and I tugged at her hair.

"I love you so much, buttercup. I could have never said no," I told her, kissing her head gently. She beamed up at me and then took a step back, looking suddenly serious. The others came over then, all the guys and Mara's grandparents.

"When can I have a baby brother or sister?" she demanded. Callan choked on the mouthful of champagne he'd just taken, and I gaped.

"Uh," I stumbled, unsure what to say.

"Give them a minute, little miss. But I'm sure in a year or so," Jason assured with a wicked grin. I was tempted to throw something at him but refrained... barely.

"I want a baby sister, please. And soon, otherwise I'll be too big, and she won't be able to do anything with me cause I'll be too busy," Mara continued. I turned to look at Callan who was grinning down at Mara and ran a hand over his hair, shaking his head.

Everyone came over to congratulate us and see the ring. My photos were put back on display and the others loaded into our car. We spoke to people for another twenty minutes before Callan tugged me aside, his fingers laced with mine.

"I can't wait to have the next few nights alone with you," he murmured before kissing me gently.

"Me too," I agreed warmly.

"And you know, little spitfire... about what Mara said... I wouldn't mind having another baby or two with you... when you're ready," he added. My heart thudded hard at the thought, and I turned to watch Mara grinning and dancing with her uncles, and something inside me melted.

"Then you and I had best get married soon, top-shelf, because I want that too. Soon," I replied. Callan grinned, his eyes darkening as he leaned forward to give me a kiss to remember.

If someone had told me a little more than a year ago that I would be engaged and a mother, I would have laughed them out of the room. But I guess destiny had plans that would not be ignored, and that included me...

Falling For the Mountain Man.

THANK YOU FOR READING!

If you want to know more about Callan's team, I'd love to hear your feedback! I've been toying with the idea of turning this into a series, so let me know what you think.

I truly hope you enjoyed this story, and please remember to leave a review. Your words are powerful, and worth so much more than you know.

Thank you!

T. Maree

ABOUT THE AUTHOR

DID YOU KNOW …

I HAVE TWO OTHER PEN NAMES?

I know that seems like overkill, but there is a method to my madness.

Books under the name **Alexis Maree** are for paranormal romances. Not everyone likes to read this genre, so I like to keep them separate.
Likewise, not everyone likes contemporary romances, so I have another pen name for those…**T. Maree.**
Then last, but certainly not least, are my sinfully sexy romances, the ones that border on the line of "*should she really put that down in print?*"
Some people don't like those kinds of spicy scenes, and so I decided to keep those separate from the rest under the name…
Luna Maree.

So, if you'd like to check out what else I've written, go onto my website:

www.thethreemarees.com
https://linktr.ee/T_Maree

T. MAREE